# THE FROG'S SADDLE HORSE
### *and*
# OTHER TALES

*Also*

TRICKY PEIK AND OTHER
PICTURE TALES

*Selected by* Jeanne B. Hardendorff

# THE FROG'S SADDLE HORSE AND OTHER TALES

❧❧❧❧

*Selected by*

Jeanne B. Hardendorff

❧❧❧❧

*Illustrated by Helen Webber*

*J. B. Lippincott Company*

PHILADELPHIA *and* NEW YORK

# ACKNOWLEDGMENTS

"Waukewa's Eagle" by James Buckham and "The Dragon and the Dragoon" by Tudor Jenks originally appeared in *St. Nicholas* magazine published by Century Co.

"The Frog's Saddle Horse" originally appeared in FOLK TALES OF ANGOLA by Heli Chatelaine, published by Houghton-Mifflin.

"Where to Lay the Blame" by Howard Pyle was previously published by Harper Bros. in THE TWILIGHT LAND.

"Tiki-Tiki-Tembo" was previously published in THROUGH STORY-LAND WITH CHILDREN, National Association of Junior Chatauquas, copyright 1924 by Fleming H. Revell, Co.

"The Baker's Neighbor," "One Grain More Than the Devil," and "A Story of Guile" are reprinted with the permission of Charles Scribner's Sons from STORIES FROM THE AMERICAS, collected and translated by Frank Henius. Copyright 1944 Charles Scribner's Sons.

"The Ferryman" reprinted by permission of Coward-McCann, Inc. from THE FERRYMAN by Claire Hutchet Bishop and Kurt Wiese. Copyright 1941.

"The Little White Cat" was previously published in THE GOLDEN SPEAR AND OTHER FAIRY TALES by Edmund Leamy. Copyright 1911 by Desmond Fitzgerald Inc., N.Y. Used by permission of David McKay Company, Inc.

"How Cats Came to Purr" was previously published by Longmans Green and Co. in THE PIGTAIL OF AH BEN LOO by John H. Bennett. Used by permission of John H. Bennett, Executor.

"The Cobbler Astrologer and the Forty Thieves" was previously published in PERSIAN FAIRY TALES by the Peter Pauper Press, Mt. Vernon, N.Y. Used by permission of the Peter Pauper Press.

"The Mouse and the Sausage" was previously published in TALES OF LAUGHTER, edited by Kate Douglas Wiggin and Nora Archibald Smith by Doubleday & Co. Inc.

"The Legend of the Palm Tree" by Margarida Estrela Bandeira-Duarte was previously published by the Ministry of Education of Brazil. Distributed by Grosset and Dunlap.

J
3 9 8
H

To *Mama*

MARGARET FARROW deGRAFFENREID

# Foreword

"THE STORY IS THE THING and the sooner it is started the better."

Children have always felt this to be true. They have cared little for the fact that the stories they like come from different countries, different continents, different cultures. They have nevertheless absorbed the fact. For tucked in many stories were words and phrases which told them it was a baker in Lima, Peru, who did a certain thing or it was in Old Japan, or that it was an Indian boy who befriended the eagle. Sometimes it was the storyteller who prefaced the telling of a story by saying that it came from Ireland, or Angola, or Persia. They also absorbed the knowledge that the peoples around the world wondered about, laughed about, and cried about the same things they did.

The story is the thing and it is the words which make the story. Children are sensitive to the sounds of words and so is the storyteller for the craft demands it.

The choice of words helps the children sense the inevitable when Choi and Tiki-Tiki-Tembo are playing "near the well, by the well, on the well," and they feel the deliberateness as well as the movement of the gardener when the story says he went "step over step, step over step into the well."

They understand from the words how difficult it would be to escape when you are guarded by "hounds with tongues of fire and claws of iron" for those hounds would indeed be "hungry and ever watchful." They recognize the giantess "with one eye in her forehead and one in her chin" for what she is—trouble.

They recognize the importance of the command of the Little White Cat when he says, "Look not to the right or the left and let no living thing touch you," or when Sulca tells the giant's daughter, "From then on, no matter what happens, you must stay motionless, quiet, silent, like a statue." The importance of the commands are in the choice of the words. They are not half-hearted; they are specific.

Words say how long ago it was—"It is so old that if all the nine lives of all the cats that have ever lived in the world were set up together in a line, the other end of it would just reach back to the time when this occurred."

Words say how it was with the fisherman as he sat waiting for his supper—"His hunger was as sharp as vinegar and his temper hot enough to fry fat."

Words make the story and the story is the thing. The story is of Cavaramacho the goat who "summoned strength from weakness"; of the dragon who suffered from "severe internal pains"; of the frog who told a preposterous tale about the elephant and made it come true. It is how the Devil gets tricked and how cats came to purr. The story is one of these and many more.

These stories have been chosen because children have liked them and they were no longer in print. Some are straight folktales; some are original tales with a folktale pattern.

It has been a pleasure to go through the different books to bring together this collection so that children and storytellers might have them for reading and telling again.

JEANNE B. HARDENDORFF

# Contents

❦❧❦❧

# THE FROG'S SADDLE HORSE
## *and*
# OTHER TALES

# The Frog's
# Saddle Horse

❧❦❧❦

ONCE UPON A TIME the Elephant and the Frog
went courting the same girl, and at last she
promised to marry the Elephant. One day the
Frog said to her: "That Elephant is nothing
but my saddle horse."

When the Elephant came to call that night
the girl said to him: "You are nothing but the
Frog's saddle horse!"

When he heard this the Elephant went off at
once and found the Frog, and asked him: "Did
you tell the girl that I am nothing but your
saddle horse?"

"Oh, no, indeed," said the Frog. "I never told
her that!"

Thereupon they both started back together
to see the girl. On the way the Frog said:
"Grandpa Elephant, I am too tired to walk any
further. Let me climb up on your back."

"Certainly," said the Elephant. "Climb up, my grandson." So the Frog climbed up on the Elephant's back. Presently he said: "Grandpa Elephant, I am afraid that I am going to fall off. Let me take some little cords and fasten them to your tusks, to hold on by."

"Certainly, my grandson," said the Elephant; and he stood still while the Frog did as he had asked. Presently the Frog spoke again: "Grandpa Elephant, please stop and let me pick a green branch so that I can keep the flies off of you."

"Certainly, my grandson," said the Elephant, and he stood quite still while the Frog broke off the branch. Pretty soon they drew near to the house where the girl lived. And when she saw them coming, the Elephant plodding patiently along with the little Frog perched on his broad back, holding the cords in one hand and waving the green branch, she came to meet them, calling out: "Mr. Elephant, you certainly are nothing but the Frog's saddle horse!"

*An Argosy of Fables*, Edited by Frederic Taber Cooper.

# Waukewa's Eagle

ONE DAY, when the Indian boy Waukewa was hunting along the mountainside, he found a young eagle with a broken wing, lying at the base of a cliff. The bird had fallen from an aery on a ledge high above and, being too young to fly, had fluttered down the cliff and injured itself so severely that it was likely to die. When Waukewa saw it he was about to drive one of his sharp arrows through its body, for the passion of the hunter was strong in him, and the eagle plunders many a fine fish from the Indian's drying-frame. But a gentler impulse came to him as he saw the young bird quivering with pain and fright at his feet, and he slowly unbent his bow, put the arrow in his quiver, and stooped over the panting eaglet. For fully a minute the wild eyes of the wounded bird and the eyes of the Indian boy, growing gentler and softer as he gazed, looked into one another. Then the struggling and panting of the young eagle ceased; the wild, frightened look passed out of its eyes, and it suffered Waukewa to pass his hand gently over its ruffled and draggled feathers. The fierce instinct to fight, to defend its threatened life, yielded to the charm of the tenderness and pity expressed in the boy's eyes; and from that moment Waukewa and the eagle were friends.

Waukewa went slowly home to his father's lodge, bearing the wounded eaglet in his arms. He carried it so gently that the broken wing gave no twinge of pain, and the bird lay perfectly still, never offering to strike with its sharp beak the hands that clasped it.

Warming some water over the fire at the lodge, Waukewa bathed the broken wing of the eagle, and bound it up with soft strips of skin. Then he made a nest of ferns and grass inside the lodge, and laid the bird in it. The boy's mother looked on with shining eyes. Her heart was very tender. From girlhood she had loved all the creatures of the woods, and it pleased her to see some of her own gentle spirit waking in the boy.

When Waukewa's father returned from hunting, he would have caught up the young eagle and wrung its neck. But the boy pleaded with him so eagerly, stooping over the captive

and defending it with his small hands, that the
stern warrior laughed and called him his "little
squaw-heart." "Keep it, then," he said, "and
nurse it until it is well. But then you must let it
go, for we will not raise up a thief in the
lodges." So Waukewa promised that when the
eagle's wing was healed and grown so that it
could fly, he would carry it forth and give it its
freedom.

It was a month—or, as the Indians say, a
moon—before the young eagle's wing had fully
mended and the bird was old enough and strong
enough to fly. And in the meantime Waukewa
cared for it and fed it daily, and the friendship
between the boy and the bird grew very strong.

But at last the time came when the willing
captive must be freed. So Waukewa carried it
far away from the Indian lodges, where none
of the young braves might see it hovering over
and be tempted to shoot their arrows at it, and
there he let it go. The young eagle rose toward
the sky in great circles, rejoicing in its freedom
and its strange, new power of flight. But when
Waukewa began to move away from the spot,
it came swooping down again; and all day long
it followed him through the woods as he
hunted. At dusk, when Waukewa shaped his
course for the Indian lodges, the eagle would

have accompanied him. But the boy suddenly slipped into a hollow tree and hid, and after a long time the eagle stopped sweeping about in search of him and flew slowly and sadly away.

Summer passed, and then winter; and spring came again, with its flowers and birds and swarming fish in the lakes and streams. Then it was that all the Indians, old and young, braves and squaws, pushed their light canoes out from shore and with spear and hook waged pleasant war against the salmon and the red-spotted trout. After winter's long imprisonment, it was such a joy to toss in the sunshine and the warm wind and catch savory fish to take the place of dried meats and corn!

Above the great falls of the Apahoqui the salmon sported in the cool, swinging current, darting under the lee of the rocks and leaping full length in the clear spring air. Nowhere else were such salmon to be speared as those which lay among the riffles at the head of the Apahoqui rapids. But only the most daring braves ventured to seek them there, for the current was strong, and should a light canoe once pass the danger point and get caught in the rush of the rapids, nothing could save it from going over the roaring falls.

Very early in the morning of a clear April day, just as the sun was rising splendidly over the mountains, Waukewa launched his canoe a half mile above the rapids of the Apahoqui, and floated downward, spear in hand, among the salmon-riffles. He was the only one of the Indian lads who dared fish above the falls. But he had been there often, and never yet had his watchful eye and his strong paddle suffered the current to carry his canoe beyond the danger point. This morning he was alone on the river, having risen long before daylight to be first at the sport.

The riffles were full of salmon, big, lusty fellows, who glided about the canoe on every side in an endless silver stream. Waukewa plunged his spear right and left, and tossed one glittering victim after another into the bark canoe. So absorbed in the sport was he that for once he did not notice when the canoe began to glide more swiftly among the rocks. But suddenly he looked up, caught his paddle, and dipped it wildly in the swirling water. The canoe swung sidewise, shivered, held its own against the torrent, and then slowly, inch by inch, began to creep upstream toward the shore. But suddenly there was a loud, cruel snap, and the paddle parted in the boy's hands, broken just above the blade! Waukewa gave a cry of despairing agony. Then he bent to the gunwale of his canoe and with the shattered blade fought desperately against the current. But it was useless. The racing torrent swept him downward; the hungry falls roared tauntingly in his ears.

Then the Indian boy knelt calmly upright in the canoe, facing the mist of the falls, and folded his arms. His young face was stern and lofty. He had lived like a brave hitherto—now he would die like one.

Faster and faster sped the doomed canoe toward the great cataract. The black rocks glided away on either side like phantoms. The roar of the terrible waters became like thunder in the boy's ears. But still he gazed calmly and sternly ahead, facing his fate as a brave Indian should. At last he began to chant the death song, which he had learned from the older braves. In a few moments all would be over. But he would come before the Great Spirit with a fearless hymn upon his lips.

Suddenly a shadow fell across the canoe. Waukewa lifted his eyes and saw a great eagle hovering over, with dangling legs, and a spread of wings that blotted out the sun. Once more the eyes of the Indian boy and the eagle met; and now it was the eagle who was master!

With a glad cry the Indian boy stood up in his canoe, and the eagle hovered lower. Now the canoe tossed up on that great swelling

wave that climbs to the cataract's edge, and the boy lifted his hands and caught the legs of the eagle. The next moment he looked down into the awful gulf of waters from its very verge. The canoe was snatched from beneath him and plunged down the black wall of the cataract; but he and the struggling eagle were floating outward and downward through the cloud of mist. The cataract roared terribly, like a wild beast robbed of its prey. The spray beat and blinded, the air rushed upward as they fell. But the eagle struggled on with his burden. He fought his way out of the mist and the flying spray. His great wings threshed the air with a whistling sound. Down, down they sank, the boy and the eagle, but ever farther from the precipice of water and the boiling whirlpool below. At length, with a fluttering plunge, the eagle dropped on a sandbar below the whirlpool, and he and the Indian boy lay there a minute, breathless and exhausted. Then the eagle slowly lifted himself, took the air under his free wings, and soared away, while the Indian boy knelt on the sand, with shining eyes following the great bird till he faded into the gray of the cliffs.

---

*Waukewa's Eagle* by James Buckham.

# The Legend of the Palm Tree

THE TRIBE was living in happiness. The sun
warmed the huts, ripening the fruits.

Sometimes the clouds covered the sun and
the rain fell, refreshing the plantations, swelling the rivers.

But after the rain the sun became very hot.
So hot that it dried up the rivers and killed the
plants and animals.

The Indians prayed and danced, begging their
God Tupan to send them rain once more, to
quench the thirst of the plants and animals.

But their prayers were in vain. The sun continued burning. . . . Indians and animals died;
the vultures came and devoured them where
they fell.

Of all the tribe there remained in the end
only two Indians and their child. Abandoning

their home, they set forth in search of a happier land.

They traveled during the whole night. For food they had only roots to chew.

The burning sun was again high in the sky, when the boy came upon a lonely palm tree waving its green branches in the desert.

Under the scant shade of this palm tree they paused to rest.

Overcome by fatigue, the parents fell asleep. Only the little boy remained awake. He was afraid. . . .

While he was praying to the God Tupan to help them he suddenly heard a voice calling him.

Looking up he saw an Indian woman in the top of the palm tree. She said to him: "My name is Carnauba. I am here to help you. Many years ago my tribe, too, suffered from the long dry season.

"I helped my people all I could. When I died the Moon changed me into this tree that I may save the stricken. Do as I advise you and you shall yet be happy.

"Cut open my trunk and quench your thirst with my sap.

"Eat my fruits and you will be hungry no more.

"Take one of my roots and cook it. Drink this medicine and it will heal you.

"Put my leaves to dry and beat them.

"From them you will get my wax, a gray and perfumed powder, with which you will light your way in the moonless nights.

"From the straw that remains, weave your hat and your mat.

"Now you must do something for me: Plant my little nuts in order that there may grow a plantation of palm trees.

"Then you may build your hut with the timber from my trunk."

The boy did everything just as the Indian woman had told him.

Some years later a large plantation of palm trees stood swaying where the desert once had been.

The young Indian, now grown to manhood, said good-bye to his parents, as he set forth to carry the Indians, near and far, the coconuts of the good Tree of Providence, as the happy natives of Brazil call it today.

---

*The Legend of the Palm Tree* by Margarida Estrela Bandeira-Duarte.

# The Baker's Neighbor

ONCE UPON A TIME, more than one hundred years ago, there lived a baker in the city of Lima, in Peru. He was a very industrious man. At night he mixed the flour and kneaded the dough and baked his bread and pastries. Every morning when the sun rose, he stood in his shop and sold his appetizing wares to the townsfolk. He loved money better than anything else in the world. His next-door neighbor was quite a different kind of man, who did not like to work too much and would rather enjoy sitting leisurely in the sun or listening to the birds, and who did not care much for money, contrary to the stingy, penny-pinching bread-and-pastry cook. The neighbor, who tried to enjoy life and take advantage of all the small and everyday joys it offered, took great pleasure in the splendid, aromatic smell of the freshly baked rolls and cakes which the early morning breeze never failed to bring to his door.

After the night's work, the baker would go

into the open air and sit down at a little table outside his house, pull out his purse, and, just as the sun rose over the horizon, he would count the money he had taken in during the preceding day. He could inspect each coin, and for more than an hour he would figure and fret and add and subtract. His jolly neighbor would get up the moment he heard the baker bang his door and come into his back yard to start his daily counting of coins. It was the signal for the neighbor also to go downstairs, lean easily against his doorframe, and inhale the fragrant odors of the freshly baked bread and rolls and cakes. He greatly enjoyed their enticing smell and fully appreciated the value and privilege of this free and daily luxury. At the same time, his eyes would rest gratefully on the first golden rays of the brilliant Peruvian sun, while his nostrils feasted their sense of smell. It was evident that he thoroughly enjoyed himself.

The baker knew full well that his neighbor was a bad customer in the shop, but that on the other hand he profited every morning by the breeze which, coming from the sea, brought him the bakery's odors. The stingy bread kneader saw his neighbor's idle posture whenever he looked up from the money piled on the table, in front of him. He never said a word, but in-

wardly he was thoroughly aroused because he saw the satisfaction on his neighbor's face. The baker always was quite angry when he thought how the result of the blending of his costly flour, sugar, raisins, and other ingredients were all enjoyed free and without charge, as far as this neighbor went, for the latter's morning pleasure, while he, the baker, had to work most of the night to provide it.

However, one fine day, the baker decided that he had stood it long enough. He could no longer silently witness how he was deprived of the fruits of his labor and cost of his supplies, without any compensation. Going to the neighbor's house, he demanded a large sum of money for the splendid odors he had daily supplied him with for many years, without ever sending a bill or collecting any money for them. The jolly fellow at first did not seem to understand the bread-and-pastry cook, but when he at last realized what it all meant, he only laughed right into the enraged baker's face. He laughed so loud and so long that all the other neighbors AND their wives came to ask what made him laugh so much. He told them his story, interrupted by his own and the others' loud guffaws. Especially the women seemed to enjoy the situation. The baker, enraged and humiliated, returned to his shop.

Soon the whole town of Lima knew of the baker's
bill for his pastry smell.

Naturally, this annoyed the baker still more.
He was not only disappointed that he had not
at least obtained some kind of a payment from
his neighbor, but was angry because he had to
stand all the chaff and the teasings of his
neighbors, AND their wives, and even their
children. When he came out of his shop to go
on an errand, the little boys and girls would
run after him. They would pretend to sniff at
his clothes and his hands, then they would run
in front of him and yell to ask him how much
he wanted for the lovely smell they had just
enjoyed. When he could not stand it any
longer, he tried once more to get some kind of
payment from the neighbor in order to close
the matter gracefully and stop his ever-increas-
ing, humiliating embarrassment. When he was
again quite unsuccessful, and on the contrary,
was laughed at and teased more than ever, he
decided to fight for the money he felt he was
entitled to. So he took his case to court.

The Judge, like most of Lima's citizens, had
heard of the baker and his complaint before it
was ever brought to court. Nevertheless, as the
laws of Peru demanded, he invited the baker to
come to court and tell his story. The Judge,

who had a great sense of humor, listened gravely and told the complainant that he would soon decide the case. The following week, keeping his promise, he ordered both the baker and the neighbor to appear in court. He ordered the latter to bring a bag containing one hundred gold coins. The news of the impending action and of the Judge's order soon spread through the whole town of Lima. The neighbor began to lose some of his gay, carefree spirits and behavior, for he was trembling lest he would have to pay for the pastry-and-bread smells he had been enjoying in the past. On the other hand, the baker already began to rub his hands, when no one was looking, and count the gold coins in his mind, and he went around happy and grinning. Inwardly, he gloated over their possession as if they were already jingling in his pocket.

At last, a week later, both were in the court. All the neighbors and many other citizens of Lima were there, too, and they all felt sorry for the jolly fellow who looked so crestfallen and sad at the smiling and beaming baker. The courtroom was humming from all the noise and talk and whispering. However, when the clerk of the court announced the entry of the Judge, they all became silent and rose. After the Judge had ordered them to be seated, he had the plaintiff and defendant swear that they would tell the truth and nothing but the truth. Then the baker was told to repeat his complaint.

The baker, feeling that he must convince the Judge that the aromatic ordors from his oven were worth at least the hundred gold coins he expected to receive, spoke for quite a while. He told all about his work, and carefully, one by one, described the flour, milk, raisins, almonds, and all the other good things which went into his breads and pastries. He then figured their costs in detail and explained how the odors the neighbor inhaled were the result of all his work and expenditure. The Judge listened gravely.

When the baker had finished his story, the Judge gave the defendant a hard look and asked him whether the morning breeze wafted these costly bakery odors daily to his house. After this was admitted by the defendant, who was by now quite downhearted, the Judge wanted to know if the freshly baked bread and rolls and pastry had a good, enjoyable or a bad, annoying smell. The neighbor of course could not but admit that the smells were very enjoyable indeed. As soon as he had thus confirmed the pleasantness of the aromatic odors, he regretted it, for the Judge now asked him to hand the bag with the hundred gold coins to the complainant. The latter, on hearing this order, nearly shouted with joy but, while he restrained his voice, he could not keep his arms from shooting right out from his body, with hands outstretched. He almost fell over the witness-stand railing, so eager was he to grab the bag and get hold of the money. When he had at last clutched and pressed it tightly to his chest, and turned to leave and go home with the precious gold, the Judge ordered him to step to a big table in front of the bench. There he was told to empty the bag, and to count the hundred coins, one by one.

The baker thought it very kind of the Judge to give him this opportunity of checking that he had not been cheated by that good-for-nothing neighbor, who had smelled his bakery's odors for years and now at last was going to pay for them. So he emptied the bag on the large polished table and began to count. The gold coins glistened in the sunshine, and jumped and gave a fine, high, pleasant metallic sound as they hit the wood. Everyone could see that the brightness of the coins and the sound of them was a feast for the eyes and music for the ears of the greedy pastry cook. The Judge and the neighbor, and all the other neighbors, and the citizens of Lima, AND their wives could plainly see with what gloating satisfaction the baker fingered each gold coin, how he could hardly get himself to drop it to pick up the next one. He was definitely and very evidently enjoying the touch of the gold, its glint and glamor, and its sound as he counted and dropped the coins one by one onto the table, each ringing good and true.

Then he lovingly put the coins back into the bag and told the Judge that there were indeed one hundred coins and that none of them were false. For this declaration he had returned to the witness stand. Before leaving the court, he also wanted to thank the Judge for his fair and wise decision. But just then, to his utter surprise and consternation, the Judge asked him to hand the bag back to the equally surprised defendant. The Judge now rose from his chair and putting on his black cap with the red ribbon, asked all those in court to stand up. They all rose, and stood, silently and expectantly, awaiting the decision. The Judge, lifting his voice, then in the name of the people of Peru, solemnly pronounced his judgment and said: "The court has heard the baker's complaint against the neighbor and the latter's admission that he did enjoy the aromatic and appetizing odors brought to his door, at sunrise, by the morning breeze. I therefore hereby declare that the case is now settled, baker. Your neighbor has smelled your pastry and bread, and you have seen and touched his gold."

At first, no one fully realized the meaning of this wise judgment. But when they did, the hush in the court was suddenly broken and everyone was laughing, crying, shouting, and congratulating the neighbor. The latter was still standing at the rail, quite dumbfounded at first, holding the bag with one hand and feeling it with the other to make quite sure that his savings had been returned to him. Then he began to laugh—to laugh loud and long and soon the whole court was laughing, except the baker. He had silently slipped out of the court, for he realized quicker than anyone else that he had lost his case. Then the clerk of the court brought down his gavel, and asked the people to be silent and to leave the court. But in front of the courthouse, they all stood and laughed and shouted until the appearance of the neighbor whom they hoisted on their shoulders. Then, joyously noisy, they carried him, gold and all, back to his house.

The baker, when he saw the procession entering his street, hid behind his curtains. He was crestfallen and, henceforth, as he could no longer stand the sight of his life-loving and easygoing neighbor at sunrise, enjoying his bakery smells more than ever, he never went out into the morning light himself. He brought the table and the chair from the yard into his house, and counted his money inside.

But from that time many of the neighbors, their friends, AND their wives came to the jolly fellow's house every morning. There they stood and laughed and gossiped and some of them even sang. They looked at the sun's golden rays and enjoyed at the same time the aromatic smells of the pastry and bread wafted gently to them by the gentle breeze. And their laughter and gaiety went straight through door and window to the baker's ears, as he sat in a dark corner and counted his money by candle-light. But the jolly neighbor himself enjoyed the morning breeze and its aroma more than ever before.

------

*Stories from the Americas*, Collected and Translated by Frank Henius.

# Tiki-Tiki-Tembo

A LONG TIME AGO, in old Japan, when a mother loved a little boy very, very much she gave him a long, long name, but when she did not love a little boy very much she gave him hardly any name at all.

Once there was a mother who had two little boys—one she loved very, very much, and so she called him,

> "Tiki-tiki-tembo
> No sa rembo
> Hari bari broohski
> Peri pen do
> Hiki pon pom
> Nichi no miano
> Dom bori ko,"

which means everything nice in Japanese. The other one she did not love at all, and she called him "Choi."

One day the two little boys were playing near the well, and by the well, and on the well, and one of the little boys fell into the well. The other little boy ran to his mother and said, "Mother, Choi has fallen into the well." "Thou knowest I am deaf, little cherry blossom, raise thy voice." "Mother, Choi has fallen into the well!" "Yet, a little louder. Thy honorable mother cannot hear thee." "Mother, Choi has fallen into the well!" "Oh, the ungrateful child! Run quickly to the gardener and tell him to take his ladder and get Choi out of the well."

So the little boy ran to the gardener and said, "Choi has fallen into the well and Mother says for you to take your ladder and get him out." So the gardener took his ladder and went step over step, step over step into the well,

picked up the little boy, and step over step, step over step, brought him out of the well, shook him, dusted him, and patted him, and stood him up on the grass a perfectly good little Japanese boy all over again.

The next day the two little boys were playing near the well, by the well, and on the well, and the other boy fell into the well. So Choi ran to his mother and said, "Mother,

> Tiki-tiki-tembo
> No sa rembo
> Hari bari broohski
> Peri pen do
> Hiki pon pom
> Nichi no miano
> Dom bori ko

has fallen into the well." "Thou knowest I am deaf, wretched child. Raise thy voice." "Mother,

> Tiki-tiki-tembo
> No sa rembo
> Hari bari broohski
> Peri pen do
> Hiki pon pom
> Nichi no miano
> Dom bori ko

has fallen into the well." "Did I not tell thee to raise thy voice? Speak louder." "Mother,

> Tiki-tiki-tembo
> No sa rembo
> Hari bari broohski
> Peri pen do
> Hiki pon pom
> Nichi no miano
> Dom bori ko

has fallen into the well."

"Oh, not my most beautiful child, heir of all I possess, my pearl from the seashell, my little cherry blossom! Run quickly to the gardener and tell him to take his ladder and get Tiki out of the well." So the little boy ran to the gardener and said, "Oh, gardener, little

> Tiki-tiki-tembo
> No sa rembo
> Hari bari broohski
> Peri pen do
> Hiki pon pom
> Nichi no miano
> Dom bori ko

has fallen into the well." "Not

Tiki-tiki-tembo
No sa rembo
Hari bari broohski
Peri pen do
Hiki pon pom
Nichi no miano
Dom bori ko?"

said the gardener. "Yes," said Choi, "little

Tiki-tiki-tembo
No sa rembo
Hari bari broohski
Peri pen do
Hiki pon pom
Nichi no miano
Dom bori ko,

and Mother says run quickly and get your ladder and get him out." So the gardener took his ladder, went step over step, step over step into the well, picked up the little boy, and step over step, step over step brought him up out of the well and onto the grass, but poor little

Tiki-tiki-tembo
No sa rembo
Hari bari broohski

> Peri pen do
> Hiki pon pom
> Nichi no miano
> Dom bori ko

never grew up to be a fine Japanese man.

And now in old Japan when a mother loves a little boy very much she does not call him,

> "Tiki-tiki-tembo
> No sa rembo
> Hari bari broohski
> Peri pen do
> Hiki pon pom
> Nichi no miano
> Dom bori ko."

She gives him a tiny little short name like Su or Foy or Wang or Sing.

---

*Through Story-Land with the Children*, National Association of Junior Chatauquas.

# The Cobbler Astrologer
# and the Forty Thieves

IN THE GREAT CITY of Isfahan lived Ahmed the cobbler, an honest and industrious man, whose wish was to pass through life quietly; and he might have done so had he not married a handsome wife who, although she had condescended to accept him as a husband, was far from being contented with his humble sphere of life.

Sittâra (such was the name of Ahmed's wife) was forever forming foolish schemes of riches and grandeur, and had, through persistent nagging and threatening, forced Ahmed into becoming an astrologer. And it was his good fortune to be the one who recovered the King's ruby which had been stolen. For the jeweler's wife confessed to Ahmed that she had stolen the ruby to punish her husband.

Soon after Ahmed had recovered the King's

ruby, it happened that the King's treasury was robbed of forty chests of gold and jewels, the greater part of the wealth of the kingdom. The high treasurer and other officers of state used all diligence to find the thieves, but in vain. The King sent for his astrologer, and declared that if the robbers were not detected by a stated time, he, as well as the principal ministers, should be put to death.

Only one day of the short period given them remained. All their search had proved fruitless, and the chief astrologer, who had made his calculations and exhausted his art to no purpose, had quite resigned himself to his fate, when one of his friends advised him to send for the wonderful cobbler, who had become so famous for his extraordinary discoveries. Two slaves were immediately sent to get Ahmed whom they commanded to go with them to their master. "You see the effects of your ambition," said the poor cobbler to his wife. "I am going to my death. The King's astrologer has heard of my pretensions, and will have me executed as an impostor."

On entering the palace of the chief astrologer, he was surprised to see that dignified person come forward to receive him, and lead him to the seat of honor, and not less so to hear himself thus addressed: "The ways of Heaven, most learned and excellent Ahmed, are unsearchable. The high are often cast down, and the low are lifted up. The whole world depends upon fate and fortune. It is my turn now to be depressed by fate; it is thine to be exalted by fortune."

His speech was here interrupted by a messenger from the King, who having heard of the cobbler's fame, desired his attendance. Poor Ahmed now concluded that it was all over with him, and followed the King's messenger, praying to God to deliver him from this peril. When Ahmed came into the King's presence, he bent his body to the ground, and wished his Majesty long life and prosperity. "Tell me, Ahmed," said the King, "who has stolen my treasure?"

"It was not one man," answered Ahmed, after thinking some time. "There were forty thieves concerned in the robbery."

"Very well," said the King, "but who were they? And what have they done with my gold and jewels?"

"These questions," said Ahmed, "I cannot now answer; but I hope to satisfy your Majesty, if you will grant me forty days to make my calculations."

"I grant you forty days," said the King, "but when they are past, if my treasure is not found, your life shall pay the forfeit."

Ahmed returned to his house well pleased; for he resolved to take advantage of the time allowed him to fly from a city where his fame was likely to be his ruin.

"Well, Ahmed," said his wife, as he entered, "what news at Court?"

"No news at all," said he, "except that I am to be put to death at the end of forty days, unless I find forty chests of gold and jewels which have been stolen from the royal treasury."

"But you will discover the thieves."

"How? By what means am I to find them?"

"By the same art which discovered the King's ruby."

"The same art!" replied Ahmed. "Foolish woman! Thou knowest that I have no art, and that I have only pretended to it for the sake of pleasing thee. But I have had sufficient skill to gain forty days, during which time we may easily escape to some other city; and with the money I now possess, and the aid of my former occupation, we may still obtain an honest livelihood."

"An honest livelihood!" repeated his lady, with scorn. "Will thy cobbling, thou mean, spiritless wretch, ever enable me to go to the Hemmâm like the wife of the chief astrologer?

Hear me, Ahmed! Think only of discovering the King's treasure. Thou hast just as good a chance of doing so as thou hadst of finding the ruby. At all events, I am determined thou shalt not escape; and shouldst thou try to run away, I will inform the King's officers, and have thee taken up and put to death, even before the forty days are expired. Thou knowest me too well, Ahmed, to doubt my keeping my word. So take courage, and endeavour to make thy fortune, and to place me in that rank of life to which my beauty entitles me."

The unhappy cobbler was dismayed at this speech; but knowing there was no hope of changing his wife's resolution, he resigned himself to his fate. "Well," said he, "your will shall be obeyed. All I desire is to pass the few remaining days of my life as comfortably as I can. You know I am no scholar, and have little skill in reckoning; so there are forty dates. Give me one of them every night after I have said my prayers, that I may put them in a jar and, by counting them, may always see how many of the few days I have to live are gone."

The lady, pleased at carrying her point, took the dates, and promised to be punctual in doing what her husband desired.

Meanwhile, the thieves who had stolen the

King's treasure, having been kept from leaving the city by fear of detection and pursuit, had received accurate information of every measure taken to discover them. One of them was among the crowd before the palace on the day the King sent for Ahmed; and hearing that the cobbler had immediately declared their exact number, he ran in a fright to his comrades, and exclaimed, "We are all found out! Ahmed, the new astrologer, has told the King that there are forty of us."

"There needed no astrologer to tell that," said the captain of the gang. "This Ahmed, with all his simple good nature, is a shrewd fellow. Forty chests having been stolen, he naturally guessed that there must be forty thieves, and he has made a good hit, that is all; still it is prudent to watch him, for he certainly has made some strange discoveries. One of us must go to-night, after dark, to the terrace of this cobbler's house, and listen to his conversation with his handsome wife; for he is said to be very fond of her and will, no doubt, tell her what success he has had in his endeavours to detect us."

Everybody approved of this scheme; and soon after nightfall one of the thieves repaired to the terrace. He arrived there just as the cobbler had finished his evening prayers, and his wife was giving him the first date. "Ah!" said Ahmed, as he took it. "There is one of the forty."

The thief, hearing these words, hastened in consternation to the gang, and told them that the moment he took his post he had been perceived by the supernatural knowledge of Ahmed, who immediately told his wife that one of them was there. The spy's tale was not believed by his hardened companions; something was imputed to his fears; he might have been mistaken;—in short, it was determined to send two men the next night at the same hour. They reached the house just as Ahmed, having finished his prayers, had received the second date, and heard him exclaim, "My dear wife, tonight there are two of them!"

The astonished thieves fled, and told their still incredulous comrades what they had heard. Three men were consequently sent the third night, four the fourth, and so on. Being afraid of venturing during the day, they always came as evening closed in, and just as Ahmed was receiving his date, hence they all in turn heard him say that which convinced them he was aware of their presence. On the last night they all went, and Ahmed exclaimed aloud, "The number is complete! Tonight the whole forty are here!"

All doubts were now removed. It was impossible that Ahmed should have discovered them by any natural means. How could he ascertain their exact number? and night after night, without ever once being mistaken? He must have learnt it by his skill in astrology. Even the captain now yielded, and decided that it was hopeless to elude a man thus gifted; he therefore advised that they make a friend of the cobbler, confess everything to him, and bribe him to secrecy with a share of the booty.

His advice was approved of, and an hour before dawn they knocked at Ahmed's door. The poor man jumped out of bed, and supposing the soldiers were come to lead him to execution, cried out, "Have patience! I know what you are come for. It is a very unjust and wicked deed."

"Most wonderful man!" said the captain, as the door was opened. "We are fully convinced that thou knowest why we are come, nor do we mean to justify the action of which thou speakest. Here are two thousand pieces of gold, which we will give thee, provided thou wilt swear to say nothing more about the matter."

"Say nothing about it!" said Ahmed. "Do you think it possible I can suffer such gross wrong and injustice without complaining, and making it known to all the world?"

"Have mercy on us!" exclaimed the thieves, falling on their knees. "Only spare our lives, and we will restore the royal treasure."

The cobbler started, rubbed his eyes to see if he were asleep or awake; and being satisfied that he was awake, and that the men before him were really the thieves, he assumed a solemn tone, and said: "Guilty men! Ye are persuaded that ye cannot escape from my penetration, which reaches unto the sun and moon, and knows the position and aspect of every star in the heavens. Your timely repentance has saved you. But ye must immediately restore all that ye have stolen. So go straightway, and carry the forty chests exactly as ye found them, and bury them a foot deep under the southern wall of the old ruined Hemmâm. If ye do this, your lives are spared; but if ye fail in the slightest degree, destruction will fall upon you and your families."

The thieves promised obedience to his commands and departed. Ahmed then fell on his knees, and returned thanks to God for this signal mark of his favor. About two hours later the royal guards came, and desired Ahmed to follow them. He said he would attend them as soon as he had taken leave of his wife, to whom he determined not to impart what had occurred until he saw the result. He bade her

farewell very affectionately; she supported herself with great fortitude on this trying occa-
sion, exhorting her husband to be of good
cheer, and said a few words about the good-
ness of Providence. But the fact was, Sittâra
fancied that if God took the worthy cobbler to
himself, her beauty might attract some new rich
husband, who would enable her to go to the
Hemmâm with as much splendor as the astrologer's lady, whose image still haunted her im-
agination.

The decrees of Heaven are just; a reward
suited to their merits awaited Ahmed and his
wife. The good man stood with a cheerful
countenance before the King, who was impa-
tient for his arrival, and immediately said,
"Ahmed, thy looks are promising; hast thou
discovered my treasure?"

"Does your Majesty require the thieves or
the treasure? The stars will only grant one or
the other," said Ahmed, looking down at his
table of astrological calculations. "Your Majesty must make your choice. I can deliver to
you either, but not both."

"I should be very sorry not to punish the
thieves," answered the King, "but if it must be
so, I choose the treasure."

"And you give the thieves a full and free
pardon?"

"I do, provided that I find my treasure untouched."

"Then," said Ahmed, "if your Majesty will follow me, the treasure shall be restored."

The King and all his nobles followed the cobbler to the ruins of the old Hemmâm. There, casting his eyes toward Heaven, Ahmed muttered some sounds which were supposed by the spectators to be magical conjurations, but which in reality were the prayers and thanksgivings of a sincere and pious heart to God for his wonderful deliverance. When his prayer was finished, he pointed to the southern wall, and requested that his Majesty would order his attendants to dig there. The work was hardly begun, when the whole forty chests were found in the same state as when stolen, with the treasurer's seal upon them still unbroken.

The King's joy knew no bounds; he embraced Ahmed, and immediately appointed him his new chief astrologer, assigned him to an apartment in the palace, and declared that he should marry his only daughter, as it was his duty to promote the man whom God had so singularly favored and had made instrumental in restoring the treasures of his kingdom. The young princess, who was more beautiful than the moon, was not dissatisfied with her father's choice; for her mind was stored with religion and virtue, and she had learnt to value beyond all earthly qualities that piety and learning which she believed Ahmed to possess.

The royal will was carried into execution as soon as formed, and Ahmed's money-loving wife was immediately divorced. The wheel of fortune had now taken a complete turn. The morning had found Ahmed in a wretched hovel, rising from a poor bed, in the expectation of losing his life; in the evening he was the lord of a rich palace, and married to the only daughter of a powerful King. But this change did not alter his character. As he had been meek and humble in adversity, he was modest and gentle in prosperity. Conscious of his own ignorance, he continued to ascribe his good fortune solely to the favor of Providence. He became daily more attached to the beautiful and virtuous princess whom he had married; and he could not help contrasting her character with that of his former wife, whom he had ceased to love, and of whose unreasonable and unfeeling vanity he was now fully sensible.

*Persian Fairy Tales.*

# The Ferryman

ONCE UPON A TIME there was a man who was a ferryman. He lived with his family in a little cottage at the far end of the Island. There he had a boat with a bit of square blue sail, a stout tiller, and a stern oar.

Every day, whatever the weather, he would ferry across the people from the Island to the Main Land and back again. There was no other way of crossing. It was not an easy way; the channel was full of reefs, currents, and countercurrents. Above all, there was the Devil's Hole where water would churn and swirl around and disappear in a funnel as if sucked at the bottom by a monstrous mouth. One had to know the way across and be able to navigate. Daniel knew the way across and he could navigate.

One day, as he had just sat down at the birthday table of his seventh child, someone knocked at the door and asked to be ferried across. The caller was a young man going to surprise his bride on the Main Land. Could he not wait a little while, asked Daniel. There he was, Daniel, just about to celebrate the fourth birthday of his seventh child. A good meal was set on the table, which did not happen often, and all the family was gathered together.

"The wind and the tide are against us," said Daniel. "It will take us two hours to cross. Surely your bride would understand."

But the young man would not have it any other way. And Daniel had to leave the good dinner and the party.

Well, that is life.

He pushed away from the shore, hoisted the blue square sail, and gripped the tiller firmly. The young man sat facing him. The water was murky, the wind was blowing hard. Daniel set the course. They were silent.

After a while Daniel remarked briefly:

"Funny! But I just cannot recall your name at all. You are not from the Island? I know everybody!"

The young man smiled and did not answer. They ran on silently, the boat tilted to one side, swishing the surface of the waves.

"But!" exclaimed Daniel suddenly, "how did

you get on the Island? I did not ferry you across!"

The young man smiled and did not answer.

They were in the middle of the channel.

The young man got up and started toward the prow of the boat. The boat nearly capsized.

"Sit down!" shrieked Daniel. "Are you crazy? Do you want us to be caught in the Devil's Hole?"

"Why not?" said the young man turning around slowly and still smiling mysteriously.

And just as he said this, Daniel's eyes fell on the rim of his trousers, and he saw the forked tip of a foot!

"Sancta Maria!" murmured Daniel, and he brought all the strength of his body to bear against the tiller. Slowly and as if reluctantly the boat veered away from the current, and, in a little while, they were running peacefully toward the shore.

"A narrow escape!" said the passenger, smiling wistfully. "Yours is hard work, isn't it?"

"Yes," said Daniel, trying to avoid looking down at the forked tip of the foot. "Hard work and little pay. Most of the time we do not have much to eat at home."

"Well," said the stranger, "I guess I owe you something special since you missed one good meal because of me."

And from under his cloak he took out a heavy tinkling bag.

"Gold," he said, "take it and be merry. Only one condition: a year from now I shall come and carry you away."

He threw the bag down, and without waiting for the boat to be made fast, he sauntered lightly onto the shore. "I will see you soon," he said cheerfully, and was gone before Daniel had had time to answer.

Well. There was the gold, plenty of it, more than enough to make the whole family comfortable for years to come. And, as far as next year was concerned, it was a long way off.

So Daniel brought the gold home and if he went on ferrying people across it was because the job was to his liking, but of worry about feeding his children he had none anymore.

And a year went by.

On the fifth birthday of his seventh child, Daniel heard a knock at the door. He opened it, and there was the Devil still smiling roguishly but with a glow of greed in his eyes.

"Are you ready?" he asked.

"Yes," answered Daniel, "only, I would like to ferry across just once more."

"Agreed," said the Devil. "It is all the same to me whether I pick you up here or across. Besides, I enjoy a ride."

So they went. Daniel pushed away from the shore; he hoisted the square blue sail and gripped the tiller firmly. The Devil sat facing him.

It was a beautiful summer day, but the wind was strong. When they were in the middle of the channel and the wind was blowing the hardest, Daniel, without the slightest warning, shifted the sail, pushed the tiller all the way and brought the boat about so swiftly and unexpectedly that the Devil lost his balance and fell into the water.

Daniel did not wait to see what was happening to him. He gave the boat all the canvas it could stand and away he flew, back to the Island. When he reached home the sun was setting and the day on which the Devil was to carry him away had passed.

And a year went by.

On the sixth birthday of his seventh child, Daniel heard a knock at the door. He opened it, and there was the Devil. He was not smiling but he was none too angry, only there was a glow of greater greed in his eyes.

"Are you ready?" he asked.

"Yes," answered Daniel, "only I would like . . ."

"No!" cut in the Devil sharply. "No more ferrying across."

"But I was not going to say that!" protested Daniel. "Oh! Well, never mind."

"What was it that you were going to say?" asked the Devil, as curious as all devils are.

"Oh! Nothing! Only that I would like to play one more game of bowling."

Now all devils love bowling. In summer it is their favorite game: they roll the balls and knock the pins. When there is a thunderstorm you hear the folks say: "Oh! Oh! the Devil is playing at ninepins."

So when Daniel mentioned bowling the Devil could not resist the suggestion.

"Agreed," said he. "It is all the same to me whether I carry you away before or after a bowling game. Besides, I enjoy bowling."

So they went. And they bowled and they bowled. And sometimes the Devil won, and sometimes Daniel won. And the sun was going down.

"Time to go," said the Devil. "Too bad! Such a nice game!"

"Yes," said Daniel, "but I wager that you cannot do it the way I can."

"What do you mean?" asked the Devil.

"I can throw the ball and knock all the pins down with my right hand while my left hand is tied behind my back."

"I am sure I can do that, too," said the Devil.

"I don't believe it," said Daniel. "It is easy to lose one's balance."

"To lose one's balance!" cried the Devil stung to the quick. "Indeed! I will show you! Tie my left hand behind my back."

Daniel tied the Devil's left hand behind his back. He tied it with a rope which went around and around the Devil's body, and he made it fast in back.

The Devil seized the ball with his right hand, he ran forward and rolled down the alley and knocked all the pins down.

"There!" he said triumphantly. "Now let us see you do it."

"No," said Daniel quietly, "I don't feel like it. You did it so well. I think I shall go home."

"Home!" cried the Devil. "My dear man, have you forgotten that we are bound for quite another place? Quick! Untie my hand that I may carry you away."

But nonchalantly Daniel strolled away. The angry Devil ran after him and tried to get hold of him. But he simply could not do it with only one hand, and finally he went away full of shame.

When Daniel reached home the sun was setting and the day on which the Devil was to carry him away had passed.

And a year went by.

On the seventh birthday of his seventh child Daniel heard a knock at the door. He opened it, and there was the Devil. He was not smiling. He looked angry and there was a glow of the greatest kind of greed in his eyes.

"Are you ready?" he asked grimly.

"Daddy! Daddy!" called the children. "Come and tell us what you bought at the fair of Sidi-Barrabah!"

"Sidi-Barrabah!" repeated the Devil. "What is that?"

"Oh, a fair, just a fair," said Daniel apologetically.

"Never heard of it!" said the Devil. "Strange! Tell me something about it."

"Gladly," said Daniel. "Won't you come in? Here is a gentleman, children, who wants to play with us."

"Play?" inquired the Devil suspiciously. "Is it a game?"

"Yes," said Daniel.

"I don't play with you anymore," said the Devil darkly.

"You do not have to play," retorted Daniel. "Watch us and you will know all about it. Are you ready, children? Then let us start:

I go to the fair of Sidi-Barrabah, and what do I buy?

A horse."

The second child went on:

"I go to the fair of Sidi-Barrabah and what do I buy?

A horse

    and a sleigh."

The third child went on:

"I go to the fair of Sidi-Barrabah and what do I buy?

A horse

a sleigh

and a top."

The fourth child went on:

"I go to the fair of Sidi-Barrabah and what do I buy?

A horse

a sleigh

a top

and a cake."

And so on until it came back to Daniel, and by that time the list of purchases to remember was quite long. And they started another round and it was more and more difficult not to forget any word. If anyone skipped or misplaced a word he lost one point, and after losing three points he was out of the game.

The Devil was intensely interested, and as the children gradually fell out and Daniel remained the winner, he said: "Let us play it, you and I. But as I do not want to be tricked again I shall set the rules down right now: there is no 'losing' point; each of us will stake his all and we shall play thirteen words, no more, no less."

"And if I win?" asked Daniel.

"You mean if you remember every word and in its right place?"

"Yes," said Daniel.

"In that case we both win, because there is not the slightest doubt that I shall be able to repeat every word, too."

"But suppose you don't," insisted Daniel.

The Devil roared with laughter.

"But it cannot be! It is impossible, unthinkable, preposterous! You will soon see why. Listen, my dear fellow, to show you how ridiculous your question is, I shall dare make a bargain with you: if I lose the game, you are free."

"Agreed," said Daniel. "Let us start:

I go to the fair of Sidi-Barrabah and what do I buy?

A whip."

The Devil: "I go to the fair of Sidi-Barrabah and what do I buy?

A whip

and a chimaera."

Daniel: "I go to the fair of Sidi-Barrabah and what do I buy?

A whip

a chimaera
and an apple pie."

The Devil: "I go to the fair of Sidi-Barrabah and what do I buy?

A whip
a chimaera
an apple pie
and a cockatoo."

Daniel: "I go to the fair of Sidi-Barrabah and what do I buy?

A whip

. . . . .

a chimaera
an apple pie

. . . . .

a cockatoo
and a cow."

The Devil: "I go to the fair of Sidi-Barrabah and what do I buy?

A whip
a chimaera
an apple pie
a cockatoo
a cow
and a fez."

Daniel: "I go to the fair of Sidi-Barrabah and what do I buy?

A whip

.  .  .  .  .
a chimaera
an apple pie
a cockatoo

.  .  .  .  .
a cow
a . . . f . . . f-ez
and a sail."

The Devil: "I go to the fair of Sidi-Barrabah and what do I buy?

A whip
a chimaera
an apple pie
a cockatoo
a cow
a fez
a sail
and
a hippopotamus."

Daniel: "I go to the fair of Sidi-Barrabah and what do I buy?

A whip
a chimaera
an apple pie
a cock . . . atoo
a cow
. . . . . . . .
a fez

a sail

a hip-po-po-ta-mus

and a bee."

The Devil: "I go to the fair of Sidi-Barrabah and what do I buy?

A whip

a chimaera

an apple pie

a cockatoo

a cow

a fez

a sail

a hippopotamus

a bee

and a scepter."

Daniel: "I go to the fair of Sidi-Barrabah and what do I buy?

A whip

a chimaera

an apple pie

a cockatoo

a cow

a fez

a sail

a hippopotamus

a bee

a . . . a . . . a . . . scepter

and a staff."

The Devil: "I go to the fair of Sidi-Barrabah and what do I buy?
A whip
a chimaera
an apple pie
a cockatoo
a cow
a fez
a sail
a hippopotamus
a bee
a scepter
a staff
and
a tiara."
Daniel: "I go to the fair of Sidi-Barrabah and what do I buy?
A whip
a chimaera
an apple pie
a cockatoo
a cow
. . . . . . .
a fez
a sail
. . . . .
a hip-po-po-ta-mus
. . . . .

a bee

. . . . .

a scepter

. . . . .

a staff

. . . . .

a tiara

. . . . .

. . . . .

and . . . and . . . and . . ."

"And what?" shouted the Devil, dancing wildly with joy, all ready to seize his prey. "And what?"

"And a Cross," said Daniel.

Then he turned to face the Devil.

But there was no one there. Daniel had said the one word that the Devil could not repeat.

The Devil had gone and he never came back.

---

*The Ferryman* by Claire Huchet Bishop and Kurt Wiese.

# A Story of Guile

◆❧◆❧◆

THE SUN WAS SHINING BRIGHTLY in the sky, through a break in a dark sea of clouds banked above the wooded hilltops, and the goat Cava-ramacho was cropping the grass that grew green among the crags. When the storm drew a cur-tain before the sun, preliminary to hurling lightning and thunder from its gloomy depths over the trembling earth and flaming heights, the goat was overcome by panic and started running over the steep slopes until the dark mouth of a cave bearded with weeds opened before him and he slipped rashly in.

Carried away by his frenzied impulse, Cava-ramacho penetrated to the rear of the grotto; there he stopped, his flanks shaking with nerv-ous terror. But soon, as his eyes became accus-tomed to the dark, he saw with unabated hor-ror a fearful personage quietly resting within the cave, and at the same time dominating its entrance. The personage was watching him with the calm indifference which comes from strength and a sense of one's own security.

Faced with the unforeseen but real danger into which he had fallen by fleeing from an imaginary one, Cavaramacho feverishly racked his brain as to how to save his life, unquestionably threatened by Yaguarete, the terrible jaguar, who was thus unexpectedly provided with his day's meal in his own mountain home.

The goat, drawing strength from weakness, began to paw the hard floor of the cave, breathing heavily every now and then with his head down, hiding his curly beard and exhibiting the whole ominous length of his curved horns. Then, assuming a defiant pose, he continued his challenging exhibition, walking to and fro with long slow strides across the back of the cave, keeping his distance from the king of wild beasts whose fearful presence he pretended to ignore.

The jaguar, stretched on the ground with his short stout forelegs in front of him, calmly watched the extravagant animal, a relative of the deer, whose unusual actions he could not understand and whose presence had not yet awakened his appetite, sated by a recent meal. He watched him fixedly with half-shut eyes whose yellow pupils gleamed softly, and sub-

consciously he considered keeping for dinner the unexpected visitor, so well nourished on the grass and fragrant herbs of the mountain slopes.

In the midst of his pacing up and down, Cavaramacho suddenly appeared to notice the presence of Yaguarete, and, pretending a certain agreeable surprise, he greeted him with an affectedly humorous and waggish air.

"Hello! So you've been here all along? I ought to have guessed it by your scent if by nothing else."

And he raised his head, the unwonted brilliance of his eyes and the formidable aspect of his horns and his quivering beard partly masking his mortal terror.

"Yes, I am here," asserted Yaguarete, "and it is quite possible that you did not know of my presence because your own scent was so strong."

And gazing fixedly at the goat while licking himself quietly with his pink tongue, he added: "And what were you looking for in my house?"

"Looking for? Why, nothing," answered Cavaramacho, blinking before the great cat's searching glance. "I was strolling through these hills, gorging myself on grass and herbs

—whose virtues keep my incomparable strength and daring—when I decided, suddenly and without deliberate intention of bothering you, to enter this pleasant refuge to escape the consequences of a sudden downpour which might have dimmed the brilliance of my lovely coat. Wasn't that all right?"

"Ah, splendid!" replied the jaguar, with the inner intention of amusing himself for a while with the picturesque creature whose exaggerated airs and posturing did not alarm him. "And how do you spend your idle time after you have eaten your fill of herbs?" he added.

"In hunting, of course."

"Ah, magnificent! We are fellow-huntsmen, then."

"Only up to a certain point. I go hunting for the pure sport of the thing, for I find it repugnant to eat the flesh I have mutilated by my sharp horns. That is where I differ from men, who organize the hunts to sate their appetites and have to be urged on by hunger or famine before they face danger. I should be happy to think that your fearlessness and heroism are not like men's in that respect. And I go hunting," the goat continued, "only to keep my courage in training. For food, I have grass, herbs, and numberless flowers and fruits, which I prefer to the palpitating flesh of my fellow creatures. Don't you prefer, for example, a branch heavily laden with sweet fruits to the neck of a pig?"

The jaguar was becoming interested, but without answering Cavaramacho's frivolous question, he asked in his turn, "And what is your favorite game?"

"The most dangerous, which puts my agility, strength, and courage to the test: I hunt the puma."

And affecting a disdainful indifference, turning away from the jaguar, he resumed his pacing with long slow strides, without even looking at the object of his greatest and inmost fears.

The jaguar raised his triangular, slender ears at the mention of his one adversary in the forest, and asked, "And how do you hunt him?"

"Very simply: I lead him on and then await his attack. When he springs on me, I stand firm and pierce his heart with both horns. To do that, one needs legs and sharp horns like mine."

"Deer have them, too."

"Ah, my friend! You do not realize that they lack my courage."

And brusquely, seeing that the storm had abated, he played his last card. Approaching the jaguar, he proposed, "Why don't we go out to hunt! I'll take the left-hand path and you the right-hand, and we'll meet at the bottom of the valley, near the man's house. There we'll join forces and see who has had the best kill."

The sly jaguar, intending to make the goat his prey as soon as he had left the cave, replied, "No, my friend. I prefer to wait for you and benefit by the fruits of your skill. You can go out alone."

And the goat, summoning the remnants of his ebbing and feigned courage, walked slowly out of the cave, expecting at every step the leap and the blow that would put an end to his unfortunate existence.

But hardly had he left the lair of the terrible butcher, when he saw, with no little surprise (from which he recovered instantly) the body of a puma stretched out, probably killed by lightning. Immediately Cavaramacho began to leap about and butt the lifeless body of the beast until Yaguarete appeared and looked at him with deep amazement.

"Did you kill him here?" the cat asked.

"And where else would I have killed him? Hardly had I come out when I discovered he was planning to surprise us and I put him out of the way without any fuss. Here he is."

And assuming an arrogant posture, he added, "I offer you my company, if you are at all afraid, and we can continue this hunt so auspiciously begun. We can go together along this path leading to the top of the hill."

"All right," agreed Yaguarete dubiously, "but we'll do as you first suggested: I'll take this downhill path and you that other one and we'll meet in the valley."

And without saying anything more, he started out at a slow trot.

They never met again.

---

*Stories from the Americas* by Frank Henius.

# The Little White Cat

◈◈◈

A LONG, LONG TIME AGO, in a valley far away, the giant Trencoss lived in a great castle, surrounded by trees that were always green. The castle had a hundred doors, and every door was guarded by a huge, shaggy hound, with tongue of fire and claws of iron, who tore to pieces anyone who went to the castle without the giant's leave. Trencoss had made war on the King of the Torrents, and, having killed the King, and slain his people, and burned his palace, he carried off his only daughter, the Princess Eileen, to the castle in the valley. Here he provided her with beautiful rooms, and appointed a hundred dwarfs, dressed in blue and yellow satin, to wait upon her, and harpers to play sweet music for her, and he gave her diamonds without number, brighter than the sun; but he would not allow her to go outside the castle, and told her if she went one step beyond its doors, the hounds, with tongues of fire and claws of iron, would tear her to pieces. A week after her arrival war broke out between the giant and the King of the Islands, and before he set out for battle, the giant sent for the Princess, and informed her that on his return he would make her his wife. When the Princess heard this she began to cry, for she would rather die than marry the giant who had slain her father.

"Crying will only spoil your bright eyes, my little Princess," said Trencoss, "and you will have to marry me whether you like it or no."

He then bade her go back to her room, and he ordered the dwarfs to give her everything she asked for while he was away, and the harpers to play the sweetest music for her. When the Princess gained her room she cried as if her heart would break. The long day passed slowly, and the night came, but brought no sleep to Eileen, and in the gray light of the morning she rose and opened the window, and looked about in every direction to see if there were any chance of escape. But the window was ever so high above the ground, and below were the hungry and ever watchful hounds. With a heavy heart she was about to close the window when she thought she saw the branches of the tree that was nearest to it mov-

ing. She looked again, and she saw a little white cat creeping along one of the branches.

"Mew!" cried the cat.

"Poor little pussy," said the Princess. "Come to me, pussy."

"Stand back from the window," said the cat, "and I will."

The Princess stepped back, and the little white cat jumped into the room. The Princess took the little cat on her lap and stroked him with her hand, and the cat raised up its back and began to purr.

"Where do you come from, and what is your name?" asked the Princess.

"No matter where I come from or what's my name," said the cat. "I am a friend of yours, and I come to help you."

"I never wanted help worse," said the Princess.

"I know that," said the cat; "and now listen to me. When the giant comes back from battle and asks you to marry him, say to him you will marry him."

"But I will never marry him," said the Princess.

"Do what I tell you," said the cat. "When he asks you to marry him, say to him you will if his dwarfs will wind for you three balls, from the fairy dew that lies on the bushes on a misty morning, as big as these," said the cat, putting his right forefoot into his ear and taking out three balls—one yellow, one red, and one blue.

"They are very small," said the Princess. "They are not much bigger than peas, and the dwarfs will not be long at their work."

"Won't they," said the cat. "It will take them a month and a day to make one, so that will take three months and three days before the balls are wound; but the giant, like you, will think they can be made in a few days, and so he will readily promise to do what you ask. He will soon find out his mistake, but he will keep his word, and will not press you to marry him until the balls are wound."

"When will the giant come back?" asked Eileen.

"He will return tomorrow afternoon," said the cat.

"Will you stay with me until then?" said the Princess. "I am very lonely."

"I cannot stay," said the cat. "I have to go away to my palace on the island on which no man ever placed his foot, and where no man but one shall ever come."

"And where is that island?" asked the Princess. "And who is the man?"

"The island is in the far-off seas where vessels never sailed; the man you will see before many days are over; and if all goes well, he will one day slay the giant Trencoss, and free you from his power."

"Ah!" sighed the Princess. "That can never be, for no weapon can wound the hundred hounds that guard the castle, and no sword can kill the giant Trencoss."

"There is a sword that will kill him," said the cat; "but I must go now. Remember what you are to say to the giant when he comes home, and every morning watch the tree on which you saw me, and if you see in the branches anyone you like better than yourself," said the cat, winking at the Princess, "throw him these three balls and leave the rest to me; but take care not to speak a single word to him, for if you do all will be lost."

"Shall I ever see you again?" asked the Princess.

"Time will tell," answered the cat, and, without saying so much as good-bye, he jumped through the window on to the tree, and in a second was out of sight.

The morrow afternoon came, and the giant Trencoss returned from battle. Eileen knew of his coming by the furious barking of the hounds, and her heart sank, for she knew that in a few moments she would be summoned to his presence. Indeed, he had hardly entered the castle when he sent for her, and told her to get ready for the wedding. The Princess tried to look cheerful, as she answered: "I will be ready as soon as you wish; but you must first promise me something."

"Ask anything you like, little Princess," said Trencoss.

"Well, then," said Eileen, "before I marry you, you must make your dwarfs wind three balls as big as these from the fairy dew that lies on the bushes on a misty morning in summer."

"Is that all?" said Trencoss, laughing. "I shall give the dwarfs orders at once, and by this time tomorrow the balls will be wound, and our wedding can take place in the evening."

"And will you leave me to myself until then?"

"I will," said Trencoss.

"On your honor as a giant?" said Eileen.

"On my honor as a giant," replied Trencoss.

The Princess returned to her rooms, and the giant summoned all his dwarfs, and he ordered them to go forth in the dawning of the morn and to gather all the fairy dew lying on the bushes, and to wind three balls—one yellow, one red, and one blue. The next morning, and the next, and the next, the dwarfs went out into the fields and searched all the hedgerows, but they could gather only as much fairy dew as would make a thread as long as a wee girl's eyelash; and so they had to go out morning after morning, and the giant fumed and threatened, but all to no purpose. He was very angry with the Princess, and he was vexed with himself that she was so much cleverer than he was, and, moreover, he saw now that the wedding could not take place as soon as he expected.

When the little white cat went away from the castle he ran as fast as he could up hill and down dale, and never stopped until he came to the Prince of the Silver River. The Prince was alone, and very sad and sorrowful he was, for he was thinking of the Princess Eileen, and wondering where she could be.

"Mew," said the cat, as he sprang softly into the room; but the Prince did not heed him. "Mew," again said the cat; but again the Prince did not heed him. "Mew," said the cat the third time, and he jumped up on the Prince's head.

"Where do you come from, and what do you want?" asked the Prince.

"I come from where you would like to be," said the cat.

"And where is that?" said the Prince.

"Oh, where is that indeed! As if I didn't know what you are thinking of, and of whom you are thinking," said the cat; "and it would be far better for you to try and save her."

"I would give my life a thousand times over for her," said the Prince.

"For whom?" said the cat, with a wink. "I named no name, your Highness," said he.

"You know very well who she is," said the Prince, "if you knew what I was thinking of; but do you know where she is?"

"She is in danger," said the cat. "She is in the castle of the giant Trencoss, in the valley beyond the mountains."

"I will set out there at once," said the Prince, "and I will challenge the giant to battle, and will slay him."

"Easier said than done," said the cat. "There is no sword made by the hands of man that can kill him, and even if you could kill him, his hundred hounds, with tongues of fire and claws of iron, would tear you to pieces."

"Then, what am I to do?" asked the Prince.

"Be said by me," said the cat. "Go to the wood that surrounds the giant's castle, and climb the high tree that's nearest to the window that looks toward the sunset, and shake the branches, and you will see what you will see. Then hold out your hat with the silver plumes, and three balls—one yellow, one red, and one blue—will be thrown into it. And then come back here as fast as you can; but speak no word, for if you utter a single word the hounds will hear you, and you shall be torn to pieces."

Well, the Prince set off at once, and after two days' journey he came to the wood around the castle, and he climbed the tree that was nearest to the window that looked toward the sunset, and he shook the branches. As he did so, the window opened and he saw the Princess Eileen, and looking lovelier than ever. He was going to call out her name, but she placed her fingers on her lips, and he remembered what the cat had told him, that he was to speak no word. In silence he held out the hat with the silver plumes, and the Princess threw into it the three balls, one after another, and blowing him a kiss, she shut the window. And well it was she did so, for at that very moment she heard the voice of the giant, who was coming back from hunting.

The Prince waited until the giant had entered the castle before he descended the tree. He set off as fast as he could. He went up hill and down dale, and never stopped until he arrived at his own palace, and there waiting for him was the little white cat.

"Have you brought the three balls?" said he.

"I have," said the Prince.

"Then follow me," said the cat.

On they went until they left the palace far behind and came to the edge of the sea.

"Now," said the cat, "unravel a thread of the red ball, hold the thread in your right hand, drop the ball into the water, and you shall see what you shall see."

The Prince did as he was told, and the ball floated out to sea, unraveling as it went, and it went on until it was out of sight.

"Pull now," said the cat.

The Prince pulled and, as he did, he saw far away something on the sea shining like silver. It came nearer and nearer, and he saw it was a little silver boat. At last it touched the strand.

"Now," said the cat, "step into this boat and it will bear you to the palace on the island on which no man has ever placed his foot—the island in the unknown seas that were never sailed by vessels made of human hands. In that palace there is a sword with a diamond hilt, and by that sword alone the giant Trencoss can be killed. There are also a hundred cakes, and it is only on eating these the hundred hounds can die. But mind what I say to you: If you eat or drink until you reach the palace of the little cat in the island in the unknown seas, you will forget the Princess Eileen."

"I will forget myself first," said the Prince, as he stepped into the silver boat, which floated away so quickly that it was soon out of sight of land.

The day passed and the night fell, and the stars shone down upon the waters, but the boat never stopped. On she went for two whole days and nights, and on the third morning the Prince saw the island in the distance, and very glad he was; for he thought it was his journey's end, and he was almost fainting with thirst and hunger. But the day passed and the island was still before him.

At long last, on the following day, he saw by the first light of the morning that he was quite close to it, and that trees laden with fruit of every kind were bending over the water. The boat sailed round and round the island, going closer and closer every round, until, at last, the drooping branches almost touched it. The sight of the fruit within his reach made the Prince hungrier and thirstier than he was before, and forgetting his promise to the little cat—not to eat anything until he entered the palace in the unknown seas—he caught one of the branches and, in a moment, was in the tree eating the delicious fruit. While he was doing so the boat floated out to sea and soon was lost to sight; but the Prince, having eaten, forgot all about it and, worse still, forgot all about the Princess in the giant's castle. When he had eaten enough he descended the tree, and, turning his back on the sea, set out straight before him. He had not gone far when he heard the sound of music, and soon after he saw a number of maidens playing on silver harps coming toward him. When they saw him they ceased playing, and cried out: "Welcome! Welcome! Prince of the Silver River, welcome to the island of fruits and flowers. Our King and Queen saw you coming over the sea, and they sent us to bring you to the palace."

The Prince went with them, and at the palace gates the King and Queen and their daughter Kathleen received him, and gave him welcome. He hardly saw the King and Queen, for his eyes were fixed on the Princess Kathleen who looked more beautiful than a flower. He thought he had never seen anyone so lovely for, of course, he had forgotten all about poor Eileen pining away in her castle prison in the lonely valley. When the King and Queen had given welcome to the Prince a great feast was spread, and all the lords and ladies of the court sat down to it, and the Prince sat between the Queen and the Princess Kathleen, and long before the feast was finished he was over head and ears in love with her. When the feast was ended the Queen ordered the ballroom to be made ready, and when night fell the dancing began, and was kept up until the morning star, and the Prince danced all night with the Princess, falling deeper and deeper in love with her every minute. Between dancing by night and feasting by day weeks went by. All the time poor Eileen in the giant's castle was counting the hours, and all this time the dwarfs were winding the balls, and a ball and a half were already wound. At last the Prince asked the King and Queen for their daughter in marriage, and they were delighted to be able to say yes, and the day was fixed for the wedding. But on the evening before the day on which it was to take place the Prince was in his room, getting ready for a dance, when he felt something rubbing against his leg and, looking down, who should he see but the little white cat. At the sight of him the Prince remembered everything, and sad and sorry he was when he thought of Eileen watching and waiting and counting the days until he returned to save her. But he was very fond of the Princess Kathleen, and so he did not know what to do.

"You can't do anything tonight," said the cat, for he knew what the Prince was thinking of, "but when morning comes go down to the sea, and look not to the right or left, and let no living thing touch you, for if you do you shall never leave the island. Drop the second ball into the water, as you did the first, and when the boat comes in step in at once. Then you may look behind you, and you shall see what you shall see, and you'll know which you love best, the Princess Eileen or the Princess Kathleen, and you can either go or stay."

The Prince didn't sleep a wink that night, and at the first glimpse of the morning he stole from the palace. When he reached the sea he threw out the ball and, when it had floated out of sight, he saw the little boat sparkling on the horizon like a newly risen star. The Prince had scarcely passed through the palace doors when he was missed, and the King and Queen and the Princess and all the lords and ladies of the court went in search of him, taking the quickest way to the sea. While the maidens with the silver harps played sweetest music, the Princess, whose voice was sweeter than any music, called on the Prince by his name and so moved his heart that he was about to look behind, when he remembered how the cat had told him he should not do so until he was in the boat. Just as it touched the shore the Princess put out her hand and almost caught the Prince's arm, but he stepped into the boat in time to save himself and it sped away like a receding wave. A loud scream caused the Prince to look round suddenly, and when he did he saw no sign of King or Queen, or Princess, or lords or ladies, but only big green serpents, with red eyes and tongues, that hissed out fire and poison as they writhed in a hundred horrible coils.

The Prince, having escaped from the enchanted island, sailed away for three days and three nights, and every night he hoped the coming morning would show him the island he was in search of. He was faint with hunger and beginning to despair, when on the fourth morning he saw in the distance an island that, in the first rays of the sun, gleamed like fire. On coming closer to it he saw that it was clad with trees, so covered with bright red berries that hardly a leaf was to be seen. Soon the boat was almost within a stone's cast of the island, and it began to sail round and round until it was well under the bending branches. The scent of the berries was so sweet that it sharpened the Prince's hunger and he longed to pluck them; but, remembering what had happened to him on the enchanted island, he was afraid to touch them. But the boat kept on sailing round and round, and at last a great wind rose from the sea and shook the branches, and the bright, sweet berries fell into the boat until it was filled with them, and they fell upon the Prince's hands, and he took up some to look at them, and as he looked the desire to eat them grew stronger, and he said to himself it would be no harm to taste one; but when he tasted it the flavor was so delicious he swallowed it and, of course, at once he forgot all about Eileen, and the boat drifted away from him and left him standing in the water.

He climbed on to the island and, having eaten enough of the berries, he set out to see what might be before him, and it was not long until he heard a great noise and a huge iron ball knocked down one of the trees in front of him, and before he knew where he was a hundred giants came running after it. When they saw the Prince they turned toward him, and one of them caught him up in his hand and held him up that all might see him. The Prince was nearly squeezed to death, and seeing this the giant put him on the ground again.

"Who are you, my little man?" asked the giant.

"I am a Prince," replied the Prince.

"Oh, you are a Prince, are you?" said the giant. "And what are you good for?" said he.

The Prince did not know, for nobody had asked him that question before.

"I know what he's good for," said an old giantess, with one eye in her forehead and one in her chin. "I know what he's good for. He's good to eat."

When the giants heard this they laughed so loud that the Prince was frightened almost to death.

"Why," said one, "he wouldn't make a mouthful."

"Oh, leave him to me," said the giantess, "and I'll fatten him up; and when he is cooked and dressed he will be a nice dainty dish for the King."

The giants, on this, gave the Prince into the hands of the old giantess. She took him home with her to the kitchen, and fed him on sugar and spice and all things nice, so that he should be a sweet morsel for the King of the Giants when he returned to the island. The poor

Prince would not eat anything at first, but the giantess held him over the fire until his feet were scorched, and then he said to himself it was better to eat than to be burnt alive.

Well, day after day passed, and the Prince grew sadder and sadder, thinking that he would soon be cooked and dressed for the King; but sad as the Prince was, he was not half as sad as the Princess Eileen in the giant's castle, watching and waiting for the Prince to return and save her.

And the dwarfs had wound two balls, and were winding a third.

At last the Prince heard from the old giantess that the King of the Giants was to return on the following day, and she said to him:

"As this is the last night you have to live, tell me if you wish for anything, for if you do your wish will be granted."

"I don't wish for anything," said the Prince, whose heart was dead within him.

"Well, I'll come back again," said the giantess, and she went away.

The Prince sat down in a corner, thinking and thinking, until he heard close to his ear a sound like "purr, purr!" He looked around, and there before him was the little white cat.

"I ought not to come to you," said the cat;

"but, indeed, it is not for your sake I come. I come for the sake of Princess Eileen. Of course, you forgot all about her and, of course, she is always thinking of you. It's always the way—

" 'Favored lovers may forget,
Slighted lovers never yet.' "

The Prince blushed with shame when he heard the name of the Princess.

" 'Tis you that ought to blush," said the cat; "but listen to me now, and remember, if you don't obey my directions this time you'll never see me again, and you'll never set your eyes on the Princess Eileen. When the old giantess comes back tell her you wish, when the morning comes, to go down to the sea to look at it for the last time. When you reach the sea you will know what to do. But I must go now, as I hear the giantess coming." And the cat jumped out of the window and disappeared.

"Well," said the giantess, when she came in, "is there anything you wish?"

"Is it true I must die tomorrow?" asked the Prince.

"It is."

"Then," said he, "I should like to go down to the sea to look at it for the last time."

"You may do that," said the giantess, "if you get up early."

"I'll be up with the lark in the light of the morning," said the Prince.

"Very well," said the giantess, and saying, "good night," she went away.

The Prince thought the night would never pass, but at last it faded away before the gray light of the dawn, and he sped down to the sea. He threw out the third ball, and before long he saw the little boat coming toward him swifter than the wind. He threw himself into it the moment it touched the shore. Swifter than the wind it bore him out to sea, and before he had time to look behind him the island of the giantess was like a faint red speck in the distance. The day passed and the night fell, and the stars looked down, and the boat sailed on, and just as the sun rose above the sea it pushed its silver prow on the golden strand of an island greener than the leaves in summer. The Prince jumped out, and went on and on until he entered a pleasant valley, at the head of which he saw a palace white as snow.

As he approached the central door it opened for him. On entering the hall he passed into several rooms without meeting with anyone; but, when he reached the principal apartment, he found himself in a circular room in which were a thousand pillars, and every pillar was of marble, and on every pillar save one, which stood in the center of the room, was a little white cat with black eyes. Ranged round the wall, from one doorjamb to the other, were three rows of precious jewels. The first was a row of brooches of gold and silver, with their pins fixed in the wall and their heads outwards; the second was a row of torques of gold and silver; and the third a row of great swords, with hilts of gold and silver. And on many tables was food of all kinds, and drinking horns filled with foaming ale.

While the Prince was looking about him the cats kept on jumping from pillar to pillar; but seeing that none of them jumped on to the pillar in the center of the room, he began to wonder why this was so when, all of a sudden and before he could guess how it came about, there right before him on the center pillar was the little white cat.

"Don't you know me?" said he.

"I do," said the Prince.

"Ah, but you don't know who I am. This is the Palace of the Little White Cat, and I am the King of the Cats. But you must be hungry, and the feast is spread."

Well, when the feast was ended, the King of the Cats called for the sword that would kill the giant Trencoss, and the hundred cakes for the hundred watchdogs.

The cats brought the sword and the cakes and laid them before the King.

"Now," said the King, "take these; you have no time to lose. Tomorrow the dwarfs will wind the last ball, and tomorrow the giant will claim the Princess for his bride. So you should go at once; but before you go take this from me to your little girl."

And the King gave him a brooch lovelier than any on the palace walls.

The King and the Prince, followed by the cats, went down to the strand, and when the Prince stepped into the boat all the cats "mewed" three times for good luck, and the Prince waved his hat three times, and the little boat sped over the waters all through the night as brightly and as swiftly as a shooting star. In the first flush of the morning it touched the strand. The Prince jumped out and went on and on, up hill and down dale, until he came to the giant's castle. When the hounds saw him they barked furiously, and bounded toward him to tear him to pieces. The Prince flung the cakes to them, and as each hound swallowed

his cake he fell dead. The Prince then struck
his shield three times with the sword which he
had brought from the Palace of the Little White
Cat.

When the giant heard the sound he cried
out: "Who comes to challenge me on my wedding day?"

The dwarfs went out to see, and, returning,
told him it was a Prince who challenged him to
battle.

The giant, foaming with rage, seized his
heaviest iron club, and rushed out to the fight.
The fight lasted the whole day, and when the
sun went down the giant said: "We have had
enough of fighting for the day. We can begin at
sunrise tomorrow."

"Not so," said the Prince. "Now or never, win
or die."

"Then take this," cried the giant, as he aimed
a blow with all his force at the Prince's head;
but the Prince, darting forward like a flash of
lightning, drove his sword into the giant's heart
and, with a groan, he fell over the bodies of the
poisoned hounds.

When the dwarfs saw the giant dead they
began to cry and tear their hair. But the Prince
told them they had nothing to fear, and he
bade them go and tell the Princess Eileen he

wished to speak with her. But the Princess had watched the battle from her window, and when she saw the giant fall she rushed out to greet the Prince, and that very night he and she and all of the dwarfs and harpers set out for the Palace of the Silver River which they reached the next morning, and from that day to this there never has been a gayer wedding than the wedding of the Prince of the Silver River and the Princess Eileen; and though she had diamonds and pearls to spare, the only jewel she wore on her wedding day was the brooch which the Prince had brought her from the Palace of the Little White Cat in the far-off seas.

---

*The Golden Spears and Other Fairy Tales* by Edmund Leamy.

# How Cats Came
# to Purr

❧✲❧✲❧

A BOY HAVING A PET CAT which he wished to feed, said to her, "Come, cat, drink this dish of cream; it will keep your fur as soft as silk, and make you purr like a coffee mill."

He had no sooner said this than the cat, with a great glare of her green eyes, bristled her tail like a gun swab, and went over the back fence, head first—pop!—as mad as a wet hen.

And this is how she came to do so:

The story is an old one—very, very old. It may be Persian; it may be not. That is of very little moment. It is so old that if all the nine lives of all the cats that have ever lived in the world were set up together in a line, the other end of it would just reach back to the time when this occurred.

And this is the story:

Many, many years ago, in a country which was quite as far from anywhere else as the entire distance thither and back, there was a huge cat that ground the coffee in the King's kitchen, and otherwise assisted with the meals.

This cat was, in truth, the actual and very father of all subsequent cats, and his name was Sooty Will, for his hair was as black as a night in a coal hole. He was ninety years old, and his mustaches were like whisk brooms. But the most singular thing about him was that in all his life he had never once purred nor humped up his back, although his master often stroked him. The fact was that he never had learned to purr, nor had any reason, so far as he knew, for humping up his back. And being the father of all the cats, there was no one to tell him how. It remained for him to acquire a reason, and from his example to devise a habit which cats have followed from that time forth, and no doubt will forever follow.

The King of the country had long been at war with one of his neighbors; but one morning he sent back a messenger to say that he had beaten his foeman at last, and that he was coming home for an early breakfast as hungry as three bears. "Have batter-cakes and coffee," he directed, "hot and plenty of 'em!"

At that the turnspits capered and yelped with glee, for batter-cakes and coffee are not cooked upon spits, and so they were free to sally forth into the streets and watch the King's homecoming in a grand parade.

But the cat sat down on his tail in the corner and looked cross. "Scat!" said he, with an angry caterwaul. "It is not fair that you should go and that I should not."

"Oh, yes, it is," said the gleeful turnspits; "turn and turnabout is fair play: you saw the rat that was killed in the parlor."

"Turnabout fair play, indeed!" cried the cat. "Then all of you get to your spits; I am sure that is turnabout!"

"Nay," said the turnspits, wagging their tails and laughing. "That is over and over again, which is not fair play. 'Tis the coffee mill that is turn and turnabout. So turn about to your mill, Sooty Will; we are off to see the King!"

With that they pranced out into the court-yard, turning handsprings, headsprings, and heel springs as they went and, after giving three hearty and vociferous cheers in a grand chorus at the bottom of the garden, went capering away for their holiday.

The cat spat on their vanishing heels, sat

down on his tail in the chimney-corner, and was very glum indeed.

Just then the cook looked in from the pantry. "Hullo!" he said gruffly. "Come, hurry up the coffee!" That was the way he always gave his orders.

The black cat's whiskers bristled. He turned to the mill with a fierce frown, his long tail going to and fro like that of a tiger in its lair; for Sooty Will had a temper like hot gunpowder, that was apt to go off sizz, whizz, bang! and no one to save the pieces. Yet, at least while the cook was by, he turned the mill furiously, as if with right goodwill.

Meantime, out in the city, a glorious day came on. The sun went buzzing up the pink-and-yellow sky with a sound like that of a walking-doll's works, or of a big Dutch clock behind a door; banners waved from the castled heights, and bugles sang from every tower; the city gates rang with the cheers of the enthusiastic crowd. Up from cellars, down from lofts, off workbenches, and out at the doors of their masters' shops, dodging the thwacks of their masters' straps, "pop-popping" like corks from the necks of so many bottles, came apprentices, shop-boys, knaves, and scullions, crying: "God save the King! Hurrah! Hurrah! Masters and work may go to Rome; our tasks shall wait on our own sweet wills; 'tis holiday when the King comes home. God save the King! Hurrah!"

Then came the procession. There were first three regiments of trumpeters, all blowing different tunes; then fifteen regiments of mounted infantry on coal-black horses, forty squadrons of green-and-blue dragoons, and a thousand drummers and fifers in scarlet and blue and gold, making a thundering din with their rootle-te-tootle-te-tootle-te-rootle; and pretty well up to the front in the ranks was the King himself, bowing and smiling to the populace, with his hand on his breast; and after him the army, all in shining armor, just enough pounded to be picturesque, miles on miles of splendid men, all bearing the trophies of glorious war, and armed with lances, and bows and arrows, falchions, morgensterns, *martels-de-fer*, and other choice implements of justifiable homicide, and the reverse, such as hautboys and sackbuts and accordions and *Dudelsacks* and Scotch bagpipes—a glorious sight!

And, as has been said before, the city gates rang with the cheers of the crowd, crimson banners waved over the city's pinnacled summits, and bugles blew, trumpets brayed, and drums beat until it seemed that wild uproar

and rich display had reached its high millennium.

The black cat turned the coffee mill. "My oh! My oh!" he said. "It certainly is not fair that those bench-legged turnspits with feet like so much leather should see the King marching home in his glory, while I, who go shod, as it were, in velvet, should hear only the sound through the scullery windows. It is not fair. It is no doubt true that 'The cat may mew, and the dog shall have his day,' but I have as much right to my day as he; and has it not been said from immemorial time that 'A cat may look at a king'? Indeed it has, quite as much as that the dog may have his day. I will not stand it; it is not fair. A cat may look at a king; and if any cat may look at a king, why, I am the cat who may. There are no other cats in the world; I am the only one. Poh! The cook may shout till his breath gives out, he cannot frighten me; for once I am going to have my fling!"

So he forthwith swallowed the coffee mill, box, handle, drawer knobs, coffee well, and all, and was off to see the King.

So far, so good. But, ah! the sad and undeniable truth, that brightest joys too soon must end! Triumphs cannot last forever, even in a land of legends. There comes a reckoning.

When the procession was past and gone, as all processions pass and go, vanishing down the shores of forgetfulness; when barons, marquises, dukes, and dons were gone, with their pennants and banners; when the last lancers had gone prancing past and were lost to sight down the circuitous avenue, Sooty Will, with drooping tail, stood by the palace gate, dejected. He was sour and silent and glum. Indeed, who would not be, with a coffee mill on his conscience? To own up the entire truth, the cat was feeling decidedly unwell. When suddenly the cook popped his head in at the scullery entry, crying, "How now, how now, you vagabonds! The war is done, but the breakfast is not. Hurry, scurry up, scamper and trot! The cakes are all cooked and are piping hot! Then why is the coffee so slow?"

The King was in the dining hall, in dressing gown and slippers, irately calling for his breakfast!

The shamefaced, guilty cat ran hastily down the scullery stairs and hid under the refrigerator, with such a deep inward sensation of remorse that he dared not look the kind cook in the face. It now really seemed to him as if everything had gone wrong with the world, especially his own insides. This anyone will readily believe who had ever swallowed a coffee mill. He began to weep copiously.

The cook came into the kitchen. "Where is the coffee?" he said. Then, catching sight of the secluded cat, he stooped, crying, "Where is the coffee?"

The cat sobbed audibly. "Someone must have come into the kitchen while I ran out to look at the King!" he gasped, for there seemed to him no way out of the scrape but by telling a plausible untruth. "Someone must have come into the kitchen and stolen it!" And with that, choking upon the handle of the mill, which projected into his throat, he burst into inarticulate sobs.

The cook, who was, in truth, a very kindhearted man, sought to reassure the poor cat. "There; it is unfortunate, very; but do not weep; thieves thrive in kings' houses!" he said, and, stooping, he began to stroke the drooping cat's back to show that he held the weeping creature blameless.

Sooty Will's heart leaped into his throat.

"Oh, oh!" he half gasped. "Oh, oh! If he rubs his great hands down my back he will feel the corners of the coffee mill through my ribs as sure as fate! Oh, oh! I am a gone cat!" And with that, in an agony of apprehension lest his

guilt and his falsehood be thus presently detected, he humped up his back as high in the
air as he could, so that the corners of the mill
might not make bumps in his sides and that the
mill might thus remain undiscovered.

But, alas! He forgot that coffee mills turn. As
he humped up his back to cover his guilt, the
coffee mill inside rolled over, and, as it rolled,
began to grind—rr-rr-rr-rr-rr-rr-rr-rr-rr-rr!

"Oh, oh! You have swallowed the mill!" cried
the cook.

"No, no," cried the cat. "I was only thinking
aloud."

At that out stepped the Genius that lived
under the Great Ovens, and, with his finger
pointed at the cat, said in a frightful voice,
husky with wood-ashes: "Miserable and pusil-
lanimous beast! By telling a falsehood to cover
a wrong you have only made bad matters
worse. For betraying man's kindness to cover
your shame, a curse shall be upon you and all
your kind until the end of the world. Whenever
men stroke you in kindness, remembrance of
your guilt shall make you hump up your back
with shame, as you did to avoid being found
out. And in order that the reason for this curse
shall never be forgotten, whenever man is kind
to a cat the sound of the grinding of a coffee

mill inside shall perpetually remind him of your guilt and shame!"

With that the Genius vanished in a cloud of smoke.

And it was even as he said. From that day Sooty Will could never abide having his back stroked without humping it up to conceal the mill within him; and never did he hump up his back but the coffee mill began slowly to grind, rr-rr-rr-rr! inside him; so that, even in the prime of life, before his declining days had come, being seized upon by a great remorse for these things which might never be amended, he retired to a home for aged and reputable cats, and there, so far as the records reveal, lived the remainder of his days in charity and repentance.

But the curse has come down even to the present day—as the Genius that lived under the Great Ovens said—and still maintains, though cats have probably forgotten the facts, and so, when stroked, hump up their backs and purr as if these actions were a matter of pride instead of being a blot upon their family record.

---

*The Pigtail of Ah Lee Ben Loo* by John Bennett.

# The Dragon and
# the Dragoon

⋘⋙⋘⋙

THERE WAS ONCE a prosperous little town that
grew up in a valley shut in by high mountains.
A road entered the valley by a narrow rocky
pass at one end, ran through the town, making
the chief street, and then climbed the mountains and led out of the valley again. There was
no way through the valley except by this road.

As the road was a highway between two
large cities, the valley town became a conve-
nient resting place for traders and travelers, and
profited by their custom.

Far up on one of the mountains overhanging
the valley lived a colony of dragons. They were
very timid creatures, and remaining amid the
rocky heights of their home, were never seen by
men. Indeed, the inhabitants of the valley would
have said there were no such creatures in exis-

tence. But as the dragons were not disturbed they increased in numbers, and soon found it a difficult matter to secure food. Then the stronger dragons drove their weaker fellows away from their native places, compelling them to seek a living elsewhere.

One young dragon happened at last to station himself in one of the passes that led into the valley where the town was situated; and, being tired by his long crawl, the dragon lay down in the highway to rest.

Soon there came a party of traders, on foot and horseback, making their way toward the town, where they expected to rest that night. While jogging along quietly, talking about the equator, suddenly they found themselves face to face with the young dragon.

There were seven travelers, and they gave seven different sorts of yell, threw down their bundles, and took to their own or their horses' heels, without arranging where to meet again.

Now it happened, the dragon being greenish in hue, that he had not been seen until the party of traders was just opposite; and consequently the fleeing traders separated into two parties. Four of them ran back toward the city they had left that morning, and three went helter-skelter down into the valley town.

As for the dragon, he was more scared than anybody; and he tried to run away, too. But, being in too much of a hurry to climb either side of the pass, he ran first after one party, and then after the other. Finding men in both directions, he returned and howled dismally. But when the poor thing's terror had worn itself out, he began to nose about among those packages the travelers had thrown away. He found several packages of raisins, three or four hams, some salted fish, and a small keg of ginger. He was very hungry, and devoured all this food without thinking of his digestion, and soon after sank into an unquiet slumber.

Meanwhile the seven travelers were relating to the citizens and villagers the awful adventure that had befallen them in the pass. The seven travelers told seven different stories, and their listeners, in carrying the report to their neighbors, freely invented whatever small details each found necessary. So by nightfall nearly every household had scared itself out of its seven senses with a mixture of a little fact and a great deal of guessing. By midnight both town and city were either dozing uneasily or were staring wide-awake with ears pricked up.

And by midnight that unhappy dragon was wide-awake, too, and struggling with a severe internal pain. As his diet until then had been mainly mountain herbs and spring water, it is not surprising that the miscellaneous bill of fare he had just eaten should disagree with him.

The dragon did not understand what was the trouble, but he soon began to yell and roar and whine and grumble.

Down in the valley below these noises rose upon the night air with a soul-freezing effect, and those citizens who had first said "Pooh!" or "Pshaw—nonsense!" were scared out of their seven wits.

The next day the Mayor summoned the town council, and held a meeting behind locked doors. The councilmen were staid, respectable merchants, but they came into the Town Hall shaking in their shoes.

"Gentlemen," said the Mayor, "an unfounded rumor has come to our ears—"

Just then a wild shriek was heard faintly in the distance, and the Mayor stopped short, turned pale, and remained silent until the echoes died away. Then he began again:

"Gentlemen—this most extraordinary occurrence, of which no doubt—" here a second wail of distress made him catch his breath; and the Mayor abruptly concluded, "How are we to get rid of this frightful creature?"

After a few moments one of the council rose and remarked as follows:

"There is no danger, I have understood, so long as the dragon is well fed. If the beast is made desperate by hunger, he may be tempted to descend into the town, and who can tell—" a third yell rose, swelled to a shriek, and died away—"who can tell, I say, what awful things he may do?"

"What can be done?" asked the Mayor.

"I advise that we send the militia with a store of provisions, and let them deposit these in the road, so the monster may not approach."

Since no other plan was proposed, a vote was taken, and the measure was adopted unanimously.

The militia grumbled, but they had to go. Armed to the teeth, they started up toward the pass, accompanied by two very heavily loaded wagons containing a choice selection of provisions. As the dragon was now feeling less disturbed, his complaints had ceased; and the militia gained in courage as they advanced. They saw no signs of the dragon, and began to believe he had fled. But when they had come near enough to see the traders' baggage torn to bits, they lost courage at once and, wheeling to the right-about, began a return march that soon became a retreat, then turned into a rout, and ended in a panic. They arrived in town in single file: the best runner first, the second next, and so on down to the drummer boy, a little fellow who couldn't get up much speed, and who ran only because the rest did.

As the wagons had been cut loose and left in the road, it was not long before the dragon discovered them. When his appetite returned, he examined the contents of the two wagons, helped himself freely, and, before many hours had passed, was again in trouble with himself, and again confiding his troubles to the mountain echoes.

When the dragon's roaring was heard for the second time, the Mayor, without waiting to convene his advisers, sent a second supply of food.

This time the soldiers didn't go further than was necessary to see the other wagons. Consequently the dragon, gaining in courage and confidence, came nearer to the town, and made a third meal.

This time, the drummer boy, who was a brave little fellow after all, became rather curious about the dragon. Instead of running away, therefore, he waited until the rest of the troop were out of sight, and then climbed a tree.

For a while nothing happened; and the drummer boy began even to get sleepy; but just about twilight the boy heard the rattling and crackling of the dragon's scales. He peered out through the leaves and saw the dragon cautiously crawling down the road toward the wagons. The boy was so startled by the sight that he gave a violent jump, and thereby knocked his drum out of its resting place in the tree.

Whack-bang—rattlety-bang! the drum fell through the branches to the ground. At the noise the timid dragon went scuttling away up the road like a frightened mouse.

"Oho!" cried the boy. "So that's the sort of a creature you are, Mr. Dragon!"

Climbing leisurely down, the drummer boy picked up his drum, slung it over his shoulder, and returned to the town, laughing quietly to himself.

But when, the next day, the dragon made a new disturbance, he was so much nearer the town that there was consternation among the citizens. They ran to the Town Hall in throngs, and insisted that measures be taken either to destroy the monster or to protect the town from his nearer approach.

After a stormy meeting at the Town Hall,

the town crier appeared and read a proclamation from the Mayor offering a rich reward to whoever could "devise, invent, or contrive" some effective "means, plan, or contrivance" that would now, "henceforth and forever more" and "without fail put an end to and abate" the "said public menace, enemy, and threat to the prosperity and welfare of the municipality."

The proclamation, in fact, wound up by promising to grant any request that might be made by the lucky man who should succeed in overcoming or getting rid of the dragon.

No sooner was the proclamation read, than the drummer boy darted out from the crier's audience and sped away home as fast as he could go. For the drummer boy had a big brother, and the Mayor had a daughter, and the big brother was in love with the Mayor's daughter, who was a lovely and accomplished young lady. But the Mayor had "frowned upon" the big brother's "suit," because the young man was only a lieutenant of dragoons, instead of a brigadier-general glittering with gold lace, with epaulets, and other trimmings.

The drummer boy hastened home and ran up to his brother's room. The big brother was trying to write verses, and making himself sadder because the verses were not proving all that he tried to make them. And the drummer boy began to tell his big brother all about the Mayor and the proclamation, and the dragon, and the drum falling out of the tree, and the dragon's running away, until the big brother was entirely bewildered.

But after a while the drummer boy succeeded in telling his story, and the big brother succeeded in understanding it. And then both put on their best hats, and ran off to the Mayor's house. They rang the bell hard, were admitted, and the lieutenant offered to rid the town of the dragon upon condition that the Mayor would promise him his chosen bride. The Mayor was not at all impressed; but he made up his mind that either the young lieutenant of dragoons would succeed in driving off the dragon, or else that the dragon would take care that he was no more bothered by the lieutenant. So he agreed to the plan, put his promise in writing, sealed it with his signet ring, and dismissed the two brothers with a feeling of relief.

Next day the lieutenant and the drummer boy set forth for the pass. They were armed only with a few giant firecrackers and a supply of matches.

When they reached the pass, the dragon,

who had learned to expect food when he saw uniforms approaching, came smilingly forward to meet them. The big brother was a little nervous, perhaps; and so, when the dragon came within about a hundred yards, he lighted one of the cannon crackers, and flung it toward the dragon.

Now, the dragon expected food; and when he saw the attractive red-paper covering of the cracker, he rushed forward and caught it eagerly in his mouth. The dragon tried to bite the cracker in two; but there was no need of that— the giant cracker came to pieces without any assistance, and the dragon was frightened almost to death by the noise of the explosion and the terrific concussion. He started to run away up the pass. But the drummer boy had meanwhile lighted another firecracker; and this was thrown so cleverly that it exploded just in front of the fleeing dragon.

Then, with an awful shriek, the dragon turned and went climbing up over the rocks. But before he could get away, the lieutenant was after him; and, overtaking the scared reptile, he seized him by the tail.

The dragon fainted from terror.

Convinced now that the dragon was an arrant coward, the lieutenant and the drummer boy cut two stout sticks, and when the dragon had recovered his senses they drove him through the town and into their back yard.

So it all ended happily. The dragon was fed upon oatmeal and rice pudding until he was quite amiable. The lieutenant married the Mayor's daughter, and was made Generalissimo and Commander in Chief of all the forces, and the drummer boy was appointed Drum Major for life, with a pension for old age. And I must say that I wish all stories turned out as satisfactorily for all concerned.

---

*The Dragon and the Dragoon* by Tudor Jenks.

# *One Grain More Than the Devil*

ONCE UPON A TIME there was an old farmer who lived with his wife and three sons in great poverty. One day the oldest boy, tired of being poor, said to his parents, "Give me your blessing, for I want to see the world and earn my living. Perhaps, with God's help, things may be better with me somewhere else. I shall try my luck."

His mother and father, half weeping, gave him their blessing, and the boy started out to see the world.

He passed through lands rich beyond anything he had ever seen, mountainous countries and flat countries and cities with countless inhabitants. But nowhere did he find work, and he was thinking of returning home when one day he came to a very large house, standing alone on a great, barren mountain.

He knocked, and a tall man with a beard like a goat's and eyes like live coals came out.

"What the dickens! What are you doing, wandering about here, earthworm?" the man said.

"I'm looking for a job," replied the lad.

"I can give you something to do. . . . But . . . can you read?"

"Read! No, sir. Since my parents are very poor, I never went to school because I never had any clean clothes."

"Good, then! You are hired."

The man with the eyes like live coals (who was really the Devil) gave the farmer boy a simple task. It was only to change the contents of three rooms full of books to three other empty rooms just like them. The books were getting moldy and the owner wanted them aired. The boy had one other duty besides that: to milk the cows kept in a barnyard next to the house, and to await the return of the owner, who was going away on a trip, with three kettles of boiling milk.

The owner came back at the end of a month.

The boy had not been able to finish more than a third of the task in that time. The Devil was annoyed and dismissed him, but gave him a hatful of gold coins, and asked him to send his other brothers to him.

Then the second brother tried his luck but he, too, proved incapable of satisfying the Devil's demands.

Finally, it was the turn of Sulca, the youngest son. He cleaned and transferred the library in four or five months. And moreover, as he could read, he not only earned his salary, but also learned a great deal (more than the Devil had learned), since he read, one after the other, all the Devil's books. All, and ONE more —one more that the Devil had not read, a huge black book, extremely old and worm-eaten.

When he had finished, Sulca awaited the return of the owner, with three kettles of boiling milk.

One afternoon the Devil, spitting sparks, arrived on his black horse. He dismounted and Sulca offered him boiling milk. The Devil drank each kettleful at a single draft, without blinking and without burning himself. Then he gave a huge sigh of satisfaction and wiped his beard with a corner of his poncho.

"What the dickens!" he exclaimed. "Have the books been moved?"

"Yes, sir."

"How much do I owe you for your work?"

"Whatever you think right, sir."

"Good. Look here, choose for yourself the saddle horse that suits you best. Take one of the mules in the barnyard, load it with two of the baskets of silver in that room, and go home in peace. And when you get there, just untie the mule and the horse, for they will return of their own accord. Now I am going to lie down and sleep for seven days and seven nights."

They said good-bye to each other, and the Devil locked himself in the rooms, but Sulca was aware, thanks to the books, with whom he would have to reckon in the future. The mule that had been suggested to him was possessed of evil spirits, and to come close to him meant being pitilessly devoured.

But Sulca knew the secret formula. He approached the monster on the right side, seized him by one ear, and shouted at him, "The Cross, Devil!" The mule, tamed, let itself be saddled and Sulca arrived safe and sound at his father's house.

And then the persecution by the Devil began.

Thanks to the treasure brought back by Sulca, the farmer's family was now wealthy; old and young spent silver like water. One day

Sulca warned his father: "See here, Father, next Sunday a rich gaucho, very well mounted, is going to come to these parts and challenge you to a race, and you must accept. But you must not race him with any of the good horses, but with a bony broken-down hack, to show your scorn for him. That hack will be I, for I know how to change myself into a horse or any other animal at will; and I am going to win the race over the rich gaucho's horse. The rich gaucho is the Devil! Accept any bets against me, and make the most of them." He continued: "After you have won, the Devil is going to offer to buy me. You will sell me, of course, for the Devil pays well, but there's just one thing I must warn you of: be careful not to sell me with the bridle on. Just as soon as the deal is closed, take off the bridle. Understand?"

"Don't worry, my boy."

Sunday came and everything happened just as Sulca had foreseen: the broken-down hack won the race, the rich gaucho paid his bets on the spot, and suggested the purchase.

Sulca's father accepted . . . and carried away by the sight of so much money, he forgot his promise and delivered his son with the bridle on.

Sulca trotted across the country ridden by

the Devil, who almost ran him through with his long spurs, and whipped him until the blood started to flow.

"Ah, miserable earthworm!" grunted Satan. "I'll teach you to read books and learn things that are none of your business."

The Devil, on the way to his own ranch, dismounted to rest for a moment at the house of a Negro who was a friend of his.

Sulca had been tied in the shade of a willow tree by a lake in front of the Negro's house. While the two friends were talking and drinking maté in the shade, a Negro servant-boy passed the horse on his way to fetch water from the lake. The miserable appearance of the poor thirsty horse moved him to compassion. He patted and stroked the horse, and then took off his bridle so that he could drink.

"What the dickens! Don't take off his bridle!" shouted the Devil, but the boy paid no attention. The horse jumped into the water and changed himself into a catfish. The Devil jumped after him and changed himself into a gilthead. The gilthead set to work to chase the catfish and was about to seize it, when the catfish, having reached the other shore, turned into a deer which ran over the mountain.

The gilthead came out of the lake and

turned into a hound which started running at full speed after the deer, but when the hound was on the point of catching it and tearing it to pieces, the deer changed into a dove. Then the hound became a hawk which soared up into the sky after its prey.

When the dove tired, it turned into a hummingbird and took refuge in the feathers of an eagle flying by. The hawk then turned into a condor, and the condor, lifting himself up to the clouds, followed the eagle until he overtook him.

The two began to fight, and as they passed over a very high tower, the hummingbird slipped away from the eagle's feathers and flew into a window. When the condor tried to squeeze after the hummingbird, Sulca, returning suddenly to his normal shape, shouted, "the Cross, Devil!" and the enormous condor vanished like smoke in the wind.

At that very moment a beautiful golden-haired Princess was looking out of the tower window. She was a giant's daughter. And when Sulca saw her and she saw Sulca, the two fell desperately in love.

Sulca spoke first and said: "I know who you are, my child. I know that your father holds you captive in this tower, and I am the one destined to free you from your terrible father, who is set on marrying you to a prince whom you hate with all your soul. The condor that was chasing me was none other than the Devil, from whose evil arts I have been able to save myself up to now because of the knowledge I learned in books. Listen to me carefully, my dear, and hear what is in store for us:

"Your father is going to fall seriously ill, and none of the physicians in these regions will be able to cure him. When he is at death's door, an aged foreign seer with a white beard will come and, calling his inexhaustible resources into play, will effect a miraculous cure.

"Your father, to reward him for that cure, will offer him half his immense fortune; but the magician, feigning great lack of interest, will refuse to accept any money in payment for his services. The giant, his pride touched, will persist in his offers until the magician will finally say: 'Since you insist, I beg you to give me the Princess's jewels, without any exception.'

"You are to agree to hand over all your jewels and when they bring you before the magician you will give him, one by one, your earrings, your bracelets, your anklets, your necklaces, your splendid diadems, and your rings. You will give him all your jewels, all but a little gold ring which you will wear on a chain around your neck; because that ring will be I. The bearded magician, not satisfied, will insist. 'There's one ring missing here,' he will say, 'the ring which the girl is wearing hidden in her bosom.'

"Only then will you untie me from the chain, but instead of putting the ring on his hand, you will throw it down so that it will roll on a table. From then on, no matter what happens, you must stay motionless, quiet, silent, like a statue. The rest is up to me.

"Now promise me that you will do just what I ask you, and as a reward for your discretion I shall confound the Devil, I shall save many souls now under a spell, and finally, I shall marry you—that is, if you love me as I love you, my fair one, light of my eyes!"

The girl willingly agreed. Sulca changed himself into a gold ring and, trembling with fear and love, she took it in her hands, white as jasmine, and hung it about her neck.

She had not long to wait before everything Sulca had said happened just as he had foretold.

And when the girl threw the ring down to roll across the table, it fell to the floor and as it fell it turned into a pomegranate. The pomegranate was broken open by the fall, and the seeds scattered over the floor like ruby beads.

When the bearded magician saw that, he immediately turned himself into a hen with chickens. The hen and the chickens began to peck at the seeds, and, when not one was left, the hen and chickens turned into a cock. Then the cock flew to the window, and, pausing on the sill, he filled the air with his song of triumph.

The Princess was on the point of falling in a faint, and she would certainly have died of grief, if one pomegranate seed had not remained hidden in her shoe. Before the cock had finished crowing, the pomegranate seed turned into a fox which, creeping out of the girl's shoe, threw himself on the cock and, in the twinkling of an eye, ate him up. Then the fox turned into Sulca and he and the Princess embraced and kissed each other with delight, like the betrothed pair that they were, and later they were married and lived happily for many years.

And that was the *extra* grain of knowledge that Sulca had gained. One grain, just one grain, more than the devil.

*Stories from the Americas* by Frank Henius.

# Where to Lay
# the Blame

MANY AND MANY a man has come to trouble—
so he will say—by following his wife's advice.
This is how it was with a man of whom I shall
tell you.

There was once upon a time a fisherman who
had fished all day long and had caught not so
much as a sprat. So at night there he sat by the
fire, rubbing his knees and warming his shins,
and waiting for supper that his wife was cooking for him, and his hunger was as sharp as
vinegar, and his temper hot enough to fry fat.
While he sat there grumbling and growling
and trying to make himself comfortable and
warm, there suddenly came a knock at the
door. The good woman opened it, and there
stood an old man, clad all in red from head to

foot, and with a snowy beard at his chin as white as winter snow.

The fisherman's wife stood gaping and staring at the strange figure, but the old man in red walked straight into the hut. "Bring your nets, fisherman," said he, "and come with me. There is something that I want you to catch for me, and if I have luck I will pay you for your fishing as never fisherman was paid before."

"Not I," said the fisherman; "I go out no more this night. I have been fishing all day long until my back is nearly broken, and have caught nothing, and now I am not such a fool as to go out and leave a warm fire and a good supper at your bidding."

But the fisherman's wife had listened to what the old man had said about paying for the job, and she was of a different mind from her husband. "Come," said she, "the old man promises to pay you well. This is not a chance to be lost, I can tell you, and my advice to you is that you go."

The fisherman shook his head. No, he would not go; he had said he would not, and he would not. But the wife only smiled and said again, "My advice to you is that you go."

The fisherman grumbled and grumbled, and swore that he would not go. The wife said nothing but one thing. She did not argue; she did not lose her temper; she only said to everything that he said, "My advice to you is that you go."

At last the fisherman's anger boiled over. "Very well," said he, spitting his words at her, "if you will drive me out into the night, I suppose I will have to go." And then he spoke the words that so many men say: "Many a man has come to trouble by following his wife's advice."

Then down he took his fur cap and up he took his nets, and off he and the old man marched through the moonlight, their shadows bobbing along like black spiders behind them.

Well, on they went, out from the town and across the fields and through the woods, until at last they came to a dreary, lonesome desert, where nothing was to be seen but gray rocks and weeds and thistles.

"Well," said the fisherman, "I have fished, man and boy, for forty-seven years, but never did I see as unlikely a place to catch anything as this."

But the old man said never a word. First of all he drew a great circle with strange figures, marking it with his finger upon the ground. Then out from under his red gown he brought a tinderbox and steel, and a little silver casket covered all over with strange figures of serpents and dragons and whatnot. He brought some sticks of spicewood from his pouch, and then he struck a light and made a fire. Out of the box he took a gray powder, which he flung upon the little blaze.

Puff! Flash! A vivid flame went up into the moonlight, and then a dense smoke as black as ink, which spread out wider and wider, far and near, till all below was darker than the darkest midnight. Then the old man began to utter strange spells and words. Presently there began a rumbling that sounded louder and louder and nearer and nearer, until it roared and bellowed like thunder. The earth rocked and swayed, and the poor fisherman shook and trembled with fear till his teeth clattered in his head.

Then suddenly the roaring and bellowing ceased, and all was still as death, though the darkness was as thick and black as ever.

"Now," said the old magician—for such he was—"now we are about to take a journey such as no one ever travelled before. Heed well what I tell you. Speak not a single word, for if you do, misfortune will be sure to happen."

"Ain't I to say anything?" said the fisherman.

"No."

"Not even 'boo' to a goose?"

"No."

"Well, that is pretty hard upon a man who likes to say his say," said the fisherman.

"And moreover," said the old man, "I must blindfold you as well."

Thereupon he took from his pocket a handkerchief, and made ready to tie it about the fisherman's eyes.

"And ain't I to see anything at all?" said the fisherman.

"No."

"Not even so much as a single feather?"

"No."

"Well, then," said the fisherman, "I wish I'd not come."

But the old man tied the handkerchief tightly around his eyes, and then he was as blind as a bat.

"Now," said the old man, "throw your leg over what you feel and hold fast."

The fisherman reached down his hand, and there felt the back of something rough and hairy. He flung his leg over it, and whisk! whizz! off he shot through the air like a skyrocket. Nothing was left for him to do but grip tightly with hands and feet and to hold fast. On they went, and on they went, until, after a great while, whatever it was that was carrying him lit upon the ground, and there the fisherman found himself standing, for that which had brought him had gone.

The old man whipped the handkerchief off his eyes, and the fisherman found himself on the shores of the sea, where there was nothing to be seen but water upon one side and rocks and naked sand upon the other.

"This is the place for you to cast your nets," said the old magician, "for if we catch nothing here we catch nothing at all."

The fisherman unrolled his nets and cast them and dragged them, and then cast them and dragged them again, but neither time caught so much as a herring. But the third time that he cast he found that he had caught something that weighed as heavy as lead. He pulled and pulled, until by and by he dragged the load ashore, and what should it be but a great chest of wood, blackened by the seawater, and covered with shells and green moss.

That was the very thing that the magician had come to fish for.

From his pouch the old man took a little golden key, which he fitted into a keyhole in the side of the chest. He threw back the lid; the fisherman looked within, and there was the prettiest little palace that man's eyes ever beheld, all made of mother-of-pearl and silver-frosted as white snow. The old magician lifted the little palace out of the box and set it upon the ground.

Then, lo and behold! A marvelous thing happened; for the palace instantly began to grow for all the world like a soap bubble, until it stood in the moonlight gleaming and glistening like snow, the windows bright with the lights of a thousand wax tapers, and the sound of music and voices and laughter coming from within.

Hardly could the fisherman catch his breath from one strange thing when another happened. The old magician took off his clothes and his face—yes, his face—for all the world as though it had been a mask, and there stood as handsome and noble a young man as ever the light looked on. Then, beckoning to the fisherman, dumb with wonder, he led the way up the great flight of marble steps to the palace door. As he came the door swung open with a blaze of light, and there stood hundreds of noblemen, all clad in silks and satins and velvets, who, when they saw the magician, bowed low before him, as though he had been a king. Leading the way, they brought the two through halls and chambers and room after room, each more magnificent than the other, until they came to one that surpassed a hundredfold any of the others.

At the farther end was a golden throne, and upon it sat a lady more lovely and beautiful than a dream, her eyes as bright as diamonds, her cheeks like rose leaves, and her hair like spun gold. She came halfway down the steps of the throne to welcome the magician, and when the two met they kissed one another before all those who were looking on. Then she brought him to the throne and seated him beside her, and there they talked for a long time very earnestly.

Nobody said a word to the fisherman, who stood staring about him like an owl. "I wonder," said he to himself at last, "if they will give a body a bite to eat by and by?" For, to tell the truth, the good supper that he had come away from at home had left a sharp hunger gnawing at his insides, and he longed for something good and warm to fill the empty place. But time passed, and not so much as a crust of bread was brought to stay his stomach.

By and by the clock struck twelve, and then the two who sat upon the throne arose. The beautiful lady took the magician by the hand and, turning to those who stood around, said, in a loud voice, "Behold him who alone is worthy to possess the jewel of jewels! Unto him do I give it, and with it all power of powers!" Thereon she opened a golden casket that stood beside her, and brought thence a little crystal ball, about as big as a pigeon's egg, in which was something that glistened like a spark of fire. The magician took the crystal ball and thrust it into his bosom; but what it was the fisherman could not guess, and if you do not know I shall not tell you.

Then for the first time the beautiful lady seemed to notice the fisherman. She beckoned him and, when he stood beside her, two men came carrying a chest. The chief treasurer opened it, and it was full of bags of gold money. "How will you have it?" said the beautiful lady.

"Have what?" said the fisherman.

"Have the pay for your labor?" said the beautiful lady.

"I will," said the fisherman promptly, "take it in my hat."

"So be it," said the beautiful lady. She waved her hand, and the chief treasurer took a bag from the chest, untied it, and emptied a cataract of gold into the fur cap. The fisherman had never seen so much wealth in all his life before, and he stood like a man turned to stone.

"Is all this mine?" said the fisherman.

"It is," said the beautiful lady.

"Then God bless your pretty eyes," said the fisherman.

Then the magician kissed the beautiful lady and, beckoning to the fisherman, left the throne room the same way that they had come. The noblemen, in silks and satins and velvets, marched ahead, and back they went through the other apartments, until at last they came to the door.

Out they stepped, and then what do you suppose happened?

If the wonderful palace had grown like a bubble, like a bubble it vanished. There the two stood on the seashore, with nothing to be seen but rocks and sand and water, and the starry sky overhead.

The fisherman shook his cap of gold, and it jingled and tinkled, and was as heavy as lead. If it was not all a dream, he was rich for life. "But anyhow," said he, "they might have given a body a bite to eat."

The magician put on his red clothes and his face again, making himself as hoary and as old as before. He took out his flint and steel, and his sticks of spicewood and his gray powder, and made a great fire and smoke just as he had done before. Then again he tied his handkerchief over the fisherman's eyes. "Remember," said he, "what I told you when we started upon our journey. Keep your mouth tight shut, for if you utter so much as a single word you are a lost man. Now throw your leg over what you feel and hold fast."

The fisherman had his net over one arm and his cap of gold in the other hand; nevertheless, there he felt the same hairy thing he had felt before. He flung his leg over it, and away he was gone through the air like a skyrocket.

Now, he had grown somewhat used to strange things by this time, so he began to think that he would like to see what sort of a creature it was upon which he was riding thus through the sky. So he contrived, in spite of his net and cap, to push up the handkerchief from over one eye. Out he peeped, and then he saw as clear as day what the strange steed was.

He was riding upon a he-goat as black as night, and in front of him was the magician riding upon just such another, his great red robe fluttering out behind him in the moonlight like huge red wings.

"Great herring and little fishes!" roared the fisherman. "It is a billy goat."

Instantly goats, old man, and all were gone

like a flash. Down fell the fisherman through the empty sky, whirling over and over and around and around like a frog. He held tightly to his net, but away flew his fur cap, the golden money falling in a shower like sparks of yellow light. Down he fell and down he fell, until his head spun like a top.

By good luck his house was just below, with its thatch of soft rushes. Into the very middle of it he tumbled, and right through the thatch —bump!—into the room below.

The good wife was in bed, snoring away for dear life; but such a noise as the fisherman made coming into the house was enough to wake the dead. Up she jumped, and there she sat, staring and winking with sleep, and with her brains as addled as a duck's egg in a thunderstorm.

"There!" said the fisherman, as he gathered himself up and rubbed his shoulder. "That is what comes of following a woman's advice!"

---

*Twilight Land* by Howard Pyle.

# The Mouse and the Sausage

ONCE UPON A TIME a little mouse and a little sausage, who loved each other like sisters, decided to live together, and made their arrangements in such a way that every day one would go to walk in the fields, or make purchases in town, while the other remained at home to keep the house.

One day, when the little sausage had prepared cabbages for dinner, the little mouse, who had come back from town with a fine appetite, enjoyed it so greatly that she exclaimed: "How delicious the cabbage is today, my dear!"

"Ah!" answered the little sausage. "That is because I popped myself into the pot while it was cooking."

On the next day, as it was her turn to prepare the meals, the little mouse said to herself: "Now I will do as much for my friend as she did for me; we will have lentils for dinner and I will jump into the pot while they are boiling," and she let the action follow the word, without reflecting that a simple sausage can do some things which are out of the reach of even the wisest mouse.

When the sausage came home, she found the house lonely and silent. She called again and again, "My little mouse! Mouse of my heart!" but no one answered. Then she went to look at the lentils boiling on the stove, and, alas! found

within the pot her good little friend, who had perished at the post of duty.

Poor mousie, with the best intentions in the world, had stayed too long at her cookery, and when she desired to climb out of the pot, had no longer the strength to do so.

And the poor sausage could never be consoled! That is why today, when you put one in the pan or on the gridiron, you will hear her weep and sigh, "M-my p-poor m-mouse! Ah, m-my p-poor m-mouse!"

---

*Tales of Laughter*, Edited by Kate Douglas Wiggin and Nora Archibald Smith.